orca
limelights

HOT
NEW
THING

Laura Langston

ORCA BOOK PUBLISHERS

Library and Archives Canada Cataloguing in Publication

Langston, Laura, 1958-, author
Hot new thing / Laura Langston.
(Orca limelights)

Issued in print and electronic formats.
ISBN 978-1-4598-0431-9 (pbk.).--ISBN 978-1-4598-0432-6 (pdf).--
ISBN 978-1-4598-0433-3 (epub)

I. Title. II. Series: Orca limelights
PS8573.A5832H68 2014   jc813'.54   C2013-906640-3
C2013-906641-1

First published in the United States, 2014
Library of Congress Control Number: 2013951379

Summary: Lily finds out that acting success in Hollywood
comes at a price she may be unwilling to pay.

MIX
Paper from
responsible sources
FSC® C004071

ANCIENT FOREST ™
FRIENDLY

*Orca Book Publishers is dedicated to preserving the environment and has
printed this book on Forest Stewardship Council® certified paper.*

Orca Book Publishers gratefully acknowledges the support for
its publishing programs provided by the following agencies:
the Government of Canada through the Canada Book Fund and the
Canada Council for the Arts, and the Province of British Columbia
through the BC Arts Council and the Book Publishing Tax Credit.

Design by Teresa Bubela
Cover photography by Getty Images

ORCA BOOK PUBLISHERS   ORCA BOOK PUBLISHERS
PO Box 5626, STN. B   PO Box 468
Victoria, BC Canada   Custer, WA USA
V8R 6S4   98240-0468

www.orcabook.com
Printed and bound in Canada.

17 16 15 14 • 4 3 2 1

For two bright lights in my life:
Corinne and Desmond. With love.

One

I almost miss my first shot at fame.

When my algebra teacher, Mr. Basi, keeps me late Friday to give me *the talk*, I panic. I have to get to the studio. I need to make the audition. I need this gig. It's a speaking part.

After the lecture, I run for the bus, dodging puddles and spray from passing cars. Why did they ask us to wear white in January? Why?

On board, I pick the driest seat I can find and protect my white jeans from wayward umbrellas and drippy bags. This commercial could be the one that totally launches my career.

Hey, Lindsay Lohan started out making commercials for pizza and Jell-O. Dakota Fanning pushed Tide.

I need this audition to be a success. All I've done lately is a single spot for some kind of salami, and I didn't even speak. Plus, the money sucked. If I earned some real cash, maybe my parents would take my acting seriously.

Reel Time is one of the biggest studios in Vancouver and takes up most of a city block. I get off at the corner, hurry past the abstract bronze sculpture at the north entrance and quickly sign in.

My friend Claire grabs my arm and propels me down the hall seconds after I push through the tinted glass security doors. "We're in a set of rooms on the fifth floor." She shoots me a quick look and comes to a sudden stop. "Whoa! What happened? You look terrible."

My heart jackknifes. "I do?" I try to peer at my reflection in the stainless-steel frame of a passing wardrobe rack, but the woman is moving too fast, and all I see is a blur of white. "Did I get splashed? Is my hair messed up?"

"No, it's your eyes. You look like somebody just died."

"I failed the algebra test."

Claire sucks in a breath. "Oh, crap."

"Yeah." We sprint past a group of women costumed in period gowns, two men having a whispered conversation and a janitor spraying the wall with lemon-scented cleaner.

Claire knows all about my parents' ultimatum. If I don't pass algebra, I have to quit Arbutus Academy. As it is, I'm expecting my dad's favorite speech later. *You need to spend less time on acting. More time on polynomials. For your future. Your career.*

A career in polynomials? Shoot me now.

"You need to find someone to help you," Claire says.

Cheat, she means. "I can't do that."

Her lips tighten. "Oh my god, Lily, grow a set. You can't do everything by the book. You'll never get anywhere." Claire has angelic blue eyes and long blond hair, but she's lifetimes away from wearing a halo. "You need to move out of your comfort zone."

"What I need is a miracle and a decent gig." The truth is, I'm desperate. Last year I booked half a dozen gigs, including a small speaking part in a TV movie of the week. This year I've had only one gig. That dumb salami. Really, how low must a girl go?

Claire heads for the main elevator and pushes the Up button. "There's a closed audition for a movie of the week going on this afternoon. Word is, Nic Mills is consulting."

"Nic Mills is here?" Mills is up there with Scorsese and Spielberg. Okay, not totally, but almost.

"Yeah, and we're going."

I tap my foot as we wait for the elevator to come. "June would never schedule us for that." Especially me. I've had so many rejections, my own agent is losing interest.

Claire leans close. "Which is why we're crashing it."

Unease prickles the back of my neck. "No way."

"Yes way. I met this guy at a club last week and he's some assistant to the producer. Or maybe the director." She wrinkles her nose. "Anyway. He's in there. I'll text once we're done with the toothpaste gig, and he'll let us in." She looks at me. "You brought an extra portfolio, didn't you?"

"Of course." I always carry extras. You never know when you'll have an opportunity. The elevator pings. "But it's a closed audition. We need an invite."

The elevator doors whoosh open. Inside are more audition hopefuls, girls who obviously signed in at the south entrance, a floor below. "Grow a set," Claire mouths as she elbows her way into a sea of white clothes.

I feel like a Q-tip squished into a box. I size up my competition. The girl on my left looks athletic. The girl beside her looks artistic. Claire is girl-next-door wholesome. Me, I look exotic. Looking exotic has its pluses, though June says it makes me harder to cast.

But today it's all about the teeth. I check them out as the elevator begins to rise. One girl has square, giraffe-like teeth and another has a mouth full of small pearls. I run my tongue over my incisors. My teeth are somewhere between the two. They'd better be bright enough. I white-stripped twice last night and again this morning.

The doors open on the fifth floor. June is waiting. She's a short pigeon-shaped woman with a helmet of dyed-black hair and perma-tanned skin. "Finally!" She shoves the call sheets into our hands. "I've filled them out. Clip your head shots and resumes to the back and go into the waiting room." She points to a nearby doorway. "They'll audition you in groups of five."

I glance at my number—twenty-six—and sneeze.

"Bless you." June turns to Claire. "The casting director wants a sweet teen look, and you do that so well. When you take a cat, choose a white Persian. That'll be lovely with your hair."

"Cats?" No wonder I'm sneezing. Which I do a second time. "Who puts cats in a toothpaste commercial?"

"Don't ask questions, dear."

I shouldn't be surprised. Once I had to pretend to smell bacon while I talked to some daisies. "I'm allergic to cats." I try to see into the room, but there's a crush of people at the door, and I can't see over their shoulders. Still. Just the thought of anything feline makes me sweat. I lift my arms away from my sides. And sweat is so not my best look.

June pushes her red glasses up. "Lily." She gives me the smile I have come to hate. The I-am-apologizing-in-advance-because-you-won't-get-chosen smile. "I wouldn't worry about the cats.

6

I doubt you'll be in the room very long. But just in case—go with the Siamese."

"Siamese?" They're the absolute worst. It has something to do with their dander. Maybe I should wait in the bathroom until it's my turn. June disappears down the hall.

It won't be that bad as long as I don't touch it. I follow Claire through the doorway. The second I see the room, my throat starts to close. It's worse than bad. It's my very own cat nightmare come to life.

The room is stupid small. Seriously, I've seen bigger playpens. And there is no ventilation, not one window. There isn't even a fan. But there are dozens and dozens of cats. Okay, a dozen. Maybe two dozen. I'm not counting. All I know is the place is a blur of cats—in laps, on the floor, playing tag with their tails. I have never been exposed to so many cats at once. And at least half of them are Siamese.

What kind of toothpaste commercial *is* this, anyway?

Claire shoves a blue-eyed, brown-tipped Siamese at me. "You take this one." She picks up a white ball of fluff. "June's right. I need a Persian."

Unblinking, the cat stares up at me. My eyes start to water. When I sneeze again, it doesn't even flinch. My shoulders tighten. Hiding in the bathroom won't cut it. I need fresh air and an antihistamine. Another audition down the drain. Damn, this day sucks. "I have to leave."

"You can't." Claire leans into me. "We've got somewhere to go after this, remember?"

The Nic Mills thing. "I can't go anywhere if my eyes are swollen shut and I cannot breathe." Choking on cat dander and disappointment, I step sideways and almost crush a cat's tail. I was so counting on this gig.

Claire rolls her eyes. "Save the theatrics for the audition."

"No. You don't understand! I can't stay." My voice is climbing, but I don't care. I back into the hallway, the Siamese still in my arms.

Claire follows. "It's just one cat. It's no big deal."

My eyes are tearing up. "Just one knife. Just one bullet. *Hello!* Just one cat." Although, truthfully, just one cat wouldn't be this bad. But a busload? Big-time bad. If I'd known, I would have taken an antihistamine or brought an EpiPen or something.

"It can't happen that fast," Claire says.

"It can, especially if I touch them." My throat's getting tighter. I cough. "I'm seriously allergic to cats."

"We'll be done in twenty minutes. Take deep breaths."

"Deep breaths could kill me."

"Oh my god, Lily, you are such a drama queen!"

I don't have the breath to argue. "This isn't drama," I wheeze. "This is my *life*." I thrust the Siamese at her. Howling in protest, the Persian jumps from Claire's arms and bolts down the hall.

I hurry to the elevator and push the button.

A tall woman wearing black comes out of the waiting room, all jangling bracelets and pursed lips. She glares at me. "What's going on? We're trying to work here."

"And I'm trying to live!" I'm getting dizzy. I need fresh air. An antihistamine. And I need to get out of my shirt. There's cat dander all over it.

"My friend is a little upset," Claire interjects.

"I'm not a little upset. I am majorly upset!" My eyes are itching, but rubbing them will only make it worse. "I'm having an allergy attack that could become an asthma attack that could kill me, and I need some help *right now*!"

The woman's face turns a scary shade of purple.

"Iris!" A short burly man comes tearing down the hall. He's wearing a denim ballcap, an ugly green Hawaiian shirt and a huge smile. "I found you!"

"Wrong flower. I'm Lily." The wheezing's getting worse. It's like having an elephant on my chest. The elevator pings. "And I am leaving before I die."

"You can't."

"Oh yeah?" The doors slide open and I step inside.

He grabs a card from his pocket. "Call me." He jabs it at my arm. "Today. Tonight. When you're feeling better."

The doors start to shut. I glance down at the card. And I cannot believe what I'm seeing. *Nic Mills.* No way. I blink my itchy, runny, swelling eyes. The letters don't change. *Nic Mills.*

I shove my foot between the elevator doors. They crash back open. "I'd love to talk to you," I gasp. "But I need to take my shirt off first."

Two

They find me a robe and an antihistamine and a big glass of water. Then they take me downstairs to a conference room with plushy brown chairs and trays of pastries and two windows and no cats. I sit at a shiny oak table with June, who has turned all maternal. Her sudden interest has less to do with my near-death experience and more to do with the fact that Nic Mills likes me, I am sure.

"Lily is my Iris!" Nic Mills smiles like a happy garden gnome.

"Who is Iris?" June has her game face on: polite and interested, fresh red lipstick to match her red glasses.

"Iris plays a small but pivotal role in my new film, *Mom's Café.*"

Mom's Café? Weird that I haven't heard of it. I keep tabs on all the shoots happening in Vancouver.

"Naomi Braithwaite was supposed to play Iris," Mills adds, "but she was injured bungee jumping and she's pulled out. Casting has come up with half a dozen replacements, but none are right. And now we're behind schedule!"

Naomi Braithwaite? I am so light-headed I can hardly breathe. Nic Mills is considering me for a Naomi Braithwaite role? He's known for doing things differently and taking chances on newbies, but still. This is huge.

"You say the girl has done summer stock?" asks the only other person in the room.

The girl. Nice. I stare at him. He's a thin guy with a goatee and sharp black eyes. He doesn't even look at me.

June's head bobbles as she stretches the truth. "Absolutely!" I was an understudy last summer and appeared exactly once. "And she comes with glowing recommendations from Arbutus Academy."

Mr. Goatee isn't buying it, I can tell. "There are casting protocols," he says.

Oh no. He's the casting director?

"We'll have to screen-test her," he adds. "We need to be sure." He shoots me a brief, distasteful glance, but I don't care. He's just said the most magical words of my entire life: *screen-test her.*

"We don't have time," Nic says. "But I'm sure. With those exotic eyes and high cheek-bones and that long black hair, she could be anything—Hawaiian or Mexican or Native American or Filipino."

"She's too tall to be Filipino," Mr. Goatee says.

People are so quick to stereotype. Some Filipinos are tall. My friend John is almost six feet.

"She passed for a Lebanese girl in a commercial last year," June adds.

And an Italian salami, I almost say. Can't forget that.

"That's my point. Iris belongs to no culture and all cultures. Like the original Eve." Nic slaps the table for emphasis. "I'm telling you, Malcolm, this girl is Iris."

For the first time in, like, forever, being half Chinese and half white is working in my favor.

"To think if I hadn't been on my way to the john," Nic adds, "I would have missed her."

I crash back to Earth. Seriously? I have been discovered by a director on a pee break?

"I want to see what she can do before we sign her on," Malcolm says.

"And I want to know more about this part." June clears her throat. "Is there nudity? Swearing? Lily's a minor and her parents are conservative."

And I want to tell them both to stop with the roadblocks. This is *Nic Mills* we're talking about. Nic Mills, who has turned three unknowns into megastars in the last five years.

"There's no nudity, nothing suggestive," Nic tells June. "Iris is a server. Most of her scenes are in the restaurant. A few are on location. There might be swearing—I can't remember."

He turns to Malcolm. "You want to see what she can do? Fine. We'll get her made up and into something orange and we'll take her downstairs for a cold reading."

I am suddenly nauseous. Cold readings suck.

Malcolm pops his briefcase and hands June a stack of pages. Sweat beads my upper lip. That's my movie script. If I ace the reading.

"Pages seventeen through twenty," he tells June. "I'll call makeup and tell them you're on your way. Studio three's on dinner break. We'll meet you there in twenty minutes."

As June and I take the elevator downstairs, I seriously feel like I am having an out-of-body experience. This situation is crazy. It's like a dream.

"It looks to me, dear, as if this Iris character is something of an oracle." June is reading the scene. "Someone who is uncommonly wise for her age." She peers at me over the top of her red glasses. "You can pretend to be wise, can't you?" She looks back down. "And funny," she adds after a minute. "Wise and funny."

I'm whisked in and out of makeup so fast it makes me dizzy and then I'm taken to wardrobe, where they can't find anything orange so they give me a pink button-down shirt to wear over my white jeans instead. Every step of the way, June is issuing orders. "Remember to relax and breathe." "Don't block your face with the script." "Move around a little." "Listen and respond."

In the studio, Nic and Malcolm are waiting. Other than a camera operator and a lighting guy, the place is deserted. Two spotlights are trained on a simple living room with a bright-red sectional, fluffy white rug and rectangular coffee table.

"You ready?" Nic asks.

"I need to read the scene first."

Iris isn't just wise, I realize when I scan the pages. She's a wise-ass. In the first-meet scene with someone named Michael, she serves him pie and insults. I read through the scene a couple of times, memorizing the lines and thinking about facial expressions, my tone of voice, what gestures I'll use.

"So." Nic rubs his hands together when I'm finished. "Okay now?"

"I think so." I focus on my breath. Slow and steady.

"Who's reading for Etienne?" June asks.

My breath stutters. There is only one Etienne in the world, but it can't be him. It. Can't. Be. "Etienne?"

"Etienne Quinn," Nic tells me. "He's playing Michael."

And just like that, my breath stops. Holy Mother of God. I may never breathe again.

Nic turns to Malcolm. "You can feed her his lines."

"Personality, not perfection," June whispers as I follow Malcolm to the stage. He says something about the living room not being the right set, but his words are like wind whistling through trees. They are background noise.

They are offering me a part opposite Etienne Quinn? The hottest guy since fire? How is this possible?

Malcolm sits on the couch. "You stand there." He points. "Pretend the coffee table is the counter. Don't worry about props and don't bother pretending to pour coffee." He crosses one leg over the other and almost yawns. "We'll just do a quick read."

His indifference infuriates me. He doesn't think I can do this. Maybe it's that, or maybe it's the thought of actually meeting—and speaking to—Etienne Quinn, but suddenly I am pumped.

"Stand by," Nic calls. He cues the camera operator.

Nerves flutter in my stomach. I can do this. I pop the top button on my shirt. I can.

When Nic says, "Rolling," I am ready.

Ignoring Malcolm's instructions, I lean over and pretend to pour coffee, making sure to keep the script away from my face and to flaunt what cleavage I have. "Let me guess. You'll have the blueberry pie with chocolate ice cream and a side of fries." I raise a brow, thrust my hip out and snap an imaginary wad of gum. Malcolm almost swallows his Adam's apple. "Am I right?"

When he flubs his "Yeah, how did you know that?" line, the flutter in my stomach dissolves. I don't know if he messed up on purpose, but instead of making me nervous, his unease fuels my confidence. He is wrong about me. I *can* do this. Five minutes of banter and pretend pie and coffee later, Nic yells, "Cut."

Hands trembling, I lower the script. My knees are shaking too. Funny, I hadn't noticed. Or maybe they just started.

Malcolm stands. Suddenly I can't look him in the eye. He flubbed his lines twice. Once he even went off script. He was trying to unnerve me, I'm sure.

He thrusts his hand out. "Congratulations." I slant him a look. Grudging admiration flashes across his face. "Looks like you have yourself a part."

Nic hurries up. "Didn't I tell you?"

"You were right," Malcolm says. "Lily is Iris."

June is at my elbow, paper and pen in hand. "How soon will you need her down there?" she asks.

"No later than next week," Nic says. "We're so far behind, we'll be cramming in rehearsals at the beginning of the day's shoot."

"Down where?" I ask.

But they're ignoring me. "Lily's underage," June reminds them. "It could take weeks to get the necessary permissions."

"I'll pull some strings," Nic says.

"We can finish things in LA if necessary," Malcolm adds.

My heart skips a beat. "LA?"

"Yes." Nic nods. "The movie's being shot in LA. That isn't a problem for you, is it?"

A problem? It's not a problem. It's an impossibility. I open my mouth, but June speaks before I can. "That's not a problem at all," she says. "LA is just fine."

Three

"**I**t's impossible," my mother tells June. I'm sitting on the couch in our living room, my hands shoved under my thighs. "Lily cannot go to Los Angeles alone, and we cannot go with her." She explains the issues: My grandmother is ill and can't be left; tax season is coming and my father can't be away from his office. "They'll have to find someone else to play the part."

I slump against the cushions. The last two hours have been a roller-coaster ride. Up, down and back up. Now down again.

June sits beside me. My mother and father are in striped wing-back chairs across from us. My grandmother is in the corner rocker, reading the paper. Sleety rain pings against the window. The scent of ginger chicken wafts in from the kitchen. Under normal circumstances, it would be cozy. Not now.

"I don't think you understand." The tips of June's ears are bright red under her helmet of black hair. "This is a huge opportunity. Lily is being offered a role in a *Nic Mills* film. The role is absolutely tailor-made for her. No nudity, nothing questionable. And she will be paid extremely well."

That has to count for something, right? My parents exchange looks.

"Believe me, things like this don't happen every day," June continues. "Mr. Mills was in town scouting and he turned down six other actresses. An hour after that, he saw Lily."

During a pee break and the worst allergy attack of my life, but hey, I'm not complaining.

"It was fate," June adds dramatically. "Truly."

My mother nods. She doesn't believe in fate, but she is too polite to disagree. Besides, she supports my acting dream 100 percent. My father, on the other hand—not so much. And now he can barely contain his skepticism. "Was it fate that made you fail the makeup test in algebra?" he asks, shooting me a look.

I flush. Oh crap.

"Mr. Basi called," my mother adds softly.

"I tried!"

My grandmother looks up from her paper. She doesn't understand English, but she knows I'm upset. I lower my voice.

"I don't get algebra. Mr. Basi said I need a tutor."

"With the money Lily will make on this movie, you could hire one," June says.

My mother looks at my father. She wants this for me, I can tell.

"Mr. Mills is shooting quickly. Lily will be gone only six weeks. She'll easily catch up when she comes home."

My parents are silent.

"She has a future in film." June directs her comments to my father. "I don't think you understand that."

I swallow a gasp.

"I don't think you understand," Dad says in a too-quiet voice that makes me freeze. "We expect Lily to go to university. For that, she needs good grades, not acting credits."

"Gord." My mother puts her hand on his arm. "Relax." My mother is short, sweet-faced and soft-spoken, but she can calm my six-foot-four father better than anyone. It's like watching a kitten bring down a lion.

"Lily can do her schoolwork there." June's gray raincoat strains across her belly when she leans forward. "And with the Latino population in LA, she might even pick up some Spanish."

"I'm more concerned with algebra," Dad says. "Besides, languages are not Lily's forte."

No kidding. I glance at my grandmother, who is reading her paper again. She's lived with us for three years, and I've only picked up half a dozen words of Mandarin. I can mimic an accent in my sleep, but my brain shuts down when I have to converse in another language.

"And schoolwork is only part of the issue," he continues. Mom sends me a sympathetic look. "You're only fifteen, Lily. You're too young to go alone. We're saying no for your own good."

"My own good? Right!" I snort. My grandmother looks up again and sets her paper aside. "I'll be sixteen in three months."

"That's still too young to go alone," Dad says.

"Uncle Mike lives in LA," I remind them. "Why can't I stay with him?" Uncle Mike is Mom's brother. I met him once when I was three. I barely remember him, but Mom emails him regularly. And my grandmother usually spends a few months a year with him and his family.

"He doesn't know you well." She shifts in her chair. "And he's busy. I couldn't ask him for help."

"That's it, then," Dad says.

The matter-of-factness of his tone is my undoing. This unbelievable, life-changing opportunity is dissolving in front of me like an ice cube melting under a heat lamp. "You don't understand! I've worked so hard for this. I never miss an acting class. I try out for every audition. I spent all of last summer hanging around being an understudy. I even played a dancing salami in a commercial. But this isn't a commercial. This is a movie! With a speaking part. A part with meaning." A part with Etienne Quinn.

Dad frowns. "Don't be so melodramatic."

Tears sting my eyes. "I'm not being melodramatic. This could be my last chance!"

"That's not true."

"Oh yeah? Then how come a year ago I had lots of opportunities and this year I've gotten almost none?" I glance at June. She doesn't look at me.

"The arts are unpredictable," Dad says. "That's why you need to focus on school. You'll have years to pursue your dream after you go to college."

My throat swells. "No, I won't. This is it for me. I feel it here." I slap my chest. "My one chance to make it big. If I pass this up, it'll be over forever. I just know it."

Suddenly, everybody talks at once. My grandmother, her dark worried eyes fixed on me, says something to Mom. Mom answers in Mandarin.

With a note of impatience, June says to Dad, "Actors wait years for breaks like this. Some go all their lives without one."

He crosses his arms. "That's not my concern."

"What if I go with her? As a chaperone?"

I glance at her. June as chaperone? She doesn't even like me that much. Or she didn't until today.

"How can you leave your business?"

Something in his tone sparks my hope. At least he's not saying no.

"I'd stay in touch with clients through email and texts. I'd take work with me. I'd network. But," she quickly adds, "my primary role would be chaperoning Lily."

My grandmother continues speaking to Mom. Dad studies June. "Where would you stay?" he asks.

"My sister has a friend in West Hollywood. She has a spare room."

Dad looks at me. The energy in the room shifts. My hope starts to dance. "I'd take school-work with me," I tell him. "I'd keep up."

He weighs my words. "I know you'd try, Lily. I do. And I want to say yes." *But.* I hear the word before he says it. "But I'm just not comfortable without a family member there to look after you. I'm sorry." His face softens. "It's just not feasible."

There's a sense of finality to his words, a not-happening flatness to his blue eyes. My last thread of hope melts away. It's done. Just like that, it's over. Tears blur my vision. I turn to June. "I'm sorry." My voice is molasses thick. "Tell Mr. Mills thanks."

I stand. I need to go to my room. I need to be alone.

"Mother says Lily must go." Mom looks at Dad. "It's a dragon year. Her lucky year." My grandmother says something in Mandarin to my father. He doesn't understand her language or her culture—and for sure he doesn't believe in lucky years or lucky money or lucky colors—but he truly cares for my grandmother.

"Tell her Lily can't go alone. Tell her there will be other lucky years." He waits for Mom to translate.

But Mom doesn't. "Mother agrees. Lily must stay with family. She will talk to Mike."

My pulse jumps. I wipe my eyes and sit back down.

"It may not be convenient for him," Dad says.

Mom translates. My grandmother answers, staring fiercely at Dad. Mom smiles slightly. "Mother says it will be most convenient for Mike. Lily can have his spare room. She'll call him after dinner."

And I'm back on the roller coaster. My grandmother beams at me from the rocker, her coffee-bean eyes gleaming in her wrinkled face. I want to rush over and give her a hug, but she is not like my Irish grandmother. The most affection she has ever shown me is an occasional pat with her small, soft hand. "Thank you, thank you! Tell Uncle Mike he won't be sorry. I promise." She doesn't understand the words, but her smile widens.

"Don't get excited, Lily. He might say no."

"No," Mom tells Dad, "he won't."

"Then it's settled," June says brightly.

I start to tremble. It's happening. It really is.

"Maybe." Dad turns to me. "But even if your uncle says yes, and even with June there, you'll have rules to follow. Homework to keep up with. A curfew. And you'll have to check in with us."

"I will." I force myself to stay calm, but it's like a thousand Pop Rocks are shooting off in my stomach.

"We'll Skype," Mom adds. "Once a week. Without fail."

"Without fail." I giggle. *Without fail.* What a silly saying. Fail isn't in my vocabulary.

I'm going to Hollywood. I'm going to act with Etienne Quinn. My dreams are coming true.

Four

Lily to Claire: OMG. 1st class on plane!! LA is amazing!! Cousin is weird. Call me asap.
Lily to Mom: At Uncle Mike's. All fine. Don't call. Going to bed. At studio early tomorrow.
Mr. Basi to Lily: Homework attached. Due tomorrow.

A noise wakes me at dawn. Startled, I peer through the darkness and see a desk I don't recognize, an unfamiliar chair. Then I remember. I'm at Uncle Mike's house in Montecito Heights. I arrived last night.

My heart thrums. Today is my first day at the studio.

Tossing back the covers, I walk across the white carpet, open the blinds and stare down the hill. Los Angeles looks like diamonds on black ink: glittering lights, tiny winking head-lights on necklaces of roads. Goosebumps rise on my arm. I really am here.

Shivering with nerves, I pull on a hoodie and kill an hour reading the script and running my lines with the iPad. It's amazing what you can do with an electronic file and a good rehearsal app. By 6:45 AM, I'm showered, dressed and anxious. I'm worried about my performance. Getting the part of Iris is a huge break—I want to do my best. But nothing has prepared me for acting opposite Etienne Quinn. Or being in a film with Brooklyn Cory. She's up there with Angelina Jolie. Only Brooklyn collects hot guys instead of kids.

I follow the smell of coffee to the kitchen. In the doorway, I stare past the stainless-steel stove, cherry cabinets and marble-topped island to a multi-level deck that offers another breath-taking view. My uncle's house is way more upscale than I expected.

My cousin Samantha looks up from the break-fast bar. "Oh." Her sharp black eyes appraise me. Maybe I should've worn something other than jeans today, although June said to keep it casual. "You're up." Like I've slept till noon. And then she smirks.

If it were Claire, I'd say, "No, I'm not up. This is my stunt double," but I cracked two jokes last night and Sam either didn't get them or has no sense of humor, so this morning I just nod.

She gestures to a nook under the microwave. "The pot on the left is decaf. The one on the right is high octane." She points at the toaster and a series of baskets at the far end of the island. "Food is there. Help yourself."

I pour coffee and grab a banana and a container of strawberry yogurt before taking the stool across from her. "Where is everybody?"

"Gone. My parents are in the office by seven." She smooths her already-smooth black pants and walks to the dishwasher. With her starchy blue shirt, lace-up shoes and china-doll haircut, Samantha looks thirty instead of seventeen. Hard to believe she's only eighteen months older than me. I search her face for something recognizable. For a clue we're related. There's nothing. Maybe because she's full Asian and I'm only half.

She pulls a key from her pocket and puts it in front of me. "Joanne forgot to give you this last night." *Joanne*? Seriously? Why not *Mom*? "It's for the front door." She pulls a slip of paper from her other pocket. "Here's the alarm code for the door in case you're home first." She turns to go. "Have a nice day."

She's so cold, I'm amazed she's not trailing ice crystals.

"What time's dinner?" I ask.

She looks over her shoulder. "Pardon?"

"What time do you guys eat?"

She blinks. "Oh. You're joining us?"

In other words: You don't really think we want you at our dinner table, do you? A chunk of banana jams in the back of my throat. I swallow and say, "I assumed so. I mean, I don't know exactly what time I'll be finished, but I figured I'd come back here." Like I have somewhere else to go.

"Of course. You're welcome to. Dinner is at six. If you can't make it, there are heat-and-serve entrées in the freezer. I'm sure you'll find something suitable."

I watch her disappear down the hall. Maybe that's what happens when you skip two grades and get fast-tracked for college at sixteen. You turn into a bitch.

* * *

"You'll be fine," June says as our driver turns in at a set of towering black gates. Up ahead I spot a massive sandstone archway framed by palm trees. And the familiar *PMP* scroll below the words *Pallas-Mills Productions*. I clutch the seat. Ohgodohgodohgod. What makes me think I can do this?

"Today will be easy," June adds. "You'll get fitted, go through makeup, do the table read. Maybe some blocking if there's time. That's all." She punches out a number on her phone.

That's all? That's enough. Sure, I've done readings and blocking before. I've done walk-throughs, too, to get camera angles and for lighting checks. For commercials and for that movie of the week. But this is different. This is the big time.

The driver rolls to a stop at the archway. "Miss Lily O'Neal," he tells the uniformed guard. "For an eight o'clock wardrobe call. June Weatherby chaperoning."

The guard looks at a clipboard. I hold my breath. What if I'm not listed? He finally looks up. "Yep, they're clear." Our car glides forward.

The place is a maze of narrow streets and squat buildings, manicured lawns and flower beds. Awe fills me when a little golf cart whips out in front of us. I swear it's Emma Stone sitting beside the driver.

"I'll do my best," June says into her cell. "I'm having lunch with a casting director today, and I'll mention your name."

When she ends the call, I ask, "You won't be having lunch with me?"

"Good Lord, no. Craft Services is hell on my stomach." The driver parks in front of a two-storey white building. "Besides, I'd only be in the way. And I need to get out and network." She grabs her bag and opens the door. "Ready?"

Nerves tight, I follow her inside and down the hall to a room crammed with people and mirrors, rolling wardrobe racks and clothes. People are shouting and talking; the noise level is stupid loud.

"Lily O'Neal is here for her fitting," June tells a thin blond.

"She's with Trish." She points to the corner. "Red hair. Wearing blue."

Trish's hair isn't red, it's pink. But she is wearing blue. And a scowl. "Oh my god. Nic told me you were small, but not this small." She grabs my wrist and propels me onto a small wooden platform. "He should have told me you were Asian. That would have been a clue. Plus, you're late."

Two minutes, max. I look at June, but she's on her phone, plugging her free ear to drown out the noise.

Trish hands me a pair of black shoes. "Size seven. Will they fit?"

I nod. "They sh—"

"Good," she interrupts. "Because we build character from the feet up." She pulls a mannequin forward. "I already altered Naomi's costume, but you're shorter and thinner than the specs your agent emailed." Heat hits the back of my neck. I thought thin was good.

She whips the tape measure around my hips, adjusts the mannequin, orders me to lift my arms. Her scowl deepens. "There's no way I can fix this today."

The flush spreads into my cheeks.

She does my waist. "Oh Lord." My bust. "Impossible." She shakes her head and checks my bust again. "I need to cut the damn costume down by a whole size!" After more adjustments to the mannequin, she hurries to the nearest wardrobe rack.

June pockets her cell phone. "Are we done?"

We? I may as well be on my own.

"Trish, *darling*," a familiar voice calls. Brooklyn Cory. I'd recognize that voice in my sleep.

The chatter in the room fades as Brooklyn swoops forward in a cloud of perfume and honey-blond hair. Massive black sunglasses hide her eyes. Flashing a diamond the size of an olive, she kisses Trish. "What fabulous creation have you dreamed up for me this time?"

Trish flips through the hangers on the rack. "One sec, Brooklyn. I need to dress Iris first."

Brooklyn's bee-stung lips turn down. "Is she here? I heard they got a nobody for the role. That's Nic for you. Where does he find these unknowns?"

I turn hot and then cold. I seriously want the floor to swallow me whole.

Trish shoves a peach-colored top and a beige skirt into my hands. "This'll have to do for today. If Nic has a problem, tell him to call me." She looks at Brooklyn. "Brooklyn, meet Iris."

"Oh." She takes off her glasses and openly appraises me. Whoa, talk about bloodshot eyes. "Hello."

Her bio claims she's thirty-five, but this close and without makeup, Brooklyn looks older. And more plastic. I step off the platform and smile. "Hi."

"Aren't you precious?" Brooklyn drawls. Trish snickers.

My smile fades. Precious? Precious is for Chihuahuas.

"Come on, Lily," June says. "We're due in makeup."

We turn to go. When we reach the door, I hear Brooklyn say, "What was Nic thinking? At least Naomi was beautiful."

Then the two women laugh.

Five

Claire to Lily: KISS EQ for me!!!!!!!! Will call 2nite 4 sure.

Mr. Basi to Lily: 4/20. Return corrections ASAP.

I shove my phone back in my pocket as we approach the hair and makeup trailer. I shouldn't have checked my messages. Like I need to worry about math too? My stomach is already knotted, thanks to Brooklyn.

Inside makeup, a stout woman with brilliant purple hair and green eye shadow is waiting for us. "You must be Lily?"

"Yes."

She gives me a warm smile. "I'm Ellen." She gestures past the four full makeup stations to the empty one at the back of the trailer. "I'm ready for you."

June touches my arm. "I'll see you tomorrow morning. Pickup at the same time."

I grip my costume like it's a lifeline. June's a pain in the ass, but at least she's a familiar one. "You aren't taking me to the soundstage?" I feel like a kid being left at school for the first time.

"I have things to do. People to see." She pats me like I am a little dog, but at least she doesn't call me precious. "Good luck with those cheeks of hers," she tells Ellen. "It doesn't matter how much weight she loses, they still have no definition."

Man. June should be the patron saint of insensitivity.

Ellen leads me past floor-to-ceiling cupboards, shelves with wigs and fake body parts, a woman having her hair blow-dried, a guy being made up to look like an alien. "Don't worry." At first I think she's talking about my cheeks, but then she adds, "Soundstage two is easy to find. I'll give you directions."

After I sit in her black swivel chair, she drapes me with a plastic robe. "Nic wants a natural look for you. Hair tied back, light makeup." She removes brushes and foam wedges from a drawer, compacts and tubes from a nearby trolley. "Your cheekbones are perfect, by the way. Don't worry about her."

It's not June I'm worried about. It's everybody else.

Ellen tests a couple of foundation shades on my chin before finding one she likes. She jots something in her notebook, then starts dabbing liquid on my face. "What other roles have you done?"

Lulled by Ellen's easy attitude and gentle touch, I relax. A few minutes later, when she's warning me to avoid the nasty bean salad on the Craft Services table, the trailer door opens. The murmur of conversation fades. My shoulders tighten. Not Brooklyn Cory again. Please, God, no.

"AJ," someone calls out. "How're you doin'?"

A lanky man in jeans, yellow high-tops and a fitted blazer high-fives a makeup artist. "Hey, man, good to see you." He gazes down the length of the trailer. "I'm here to see Ms. Lily O'Neal."

I grip the sides of the chair. Who is this guy?

Ellen points. "Here."

Slowly he makes his way toward us, stopping at each station to talk, ask questions, crack a joke.

"AJ does PR for Nic Mills and some of the other directors," Ellen whispers when she sees me staring.

PR? I chew the corner of my lip. Why does he need to talk to me?

"Ellen, you sweet thing," he drawls as he approaches, "you're looking especially hot today."

"I always look hot," she says, but her tone is indulgent and she winks at me.

"Too true, dollface." AJ turns to me. "Ms. Lily O'Neal, I am most pleased to meet you." His formality and exaggerated southern accent make me smile.

"Mr. Mills wants to issue a media release about you taking over Ms. Braithwaite's role, and I'm the lucky guy writing it."

Me in a media release? Whoa.

He pulls a blue pen and tiny coiled notepad from his jacket pocket. "Nic told me to contact"— he looks down—"June Weatherby, but she hasn't answered my emails or returned my calls, and Nic wants the release out this afternoon."

Unease skitters down my spine. I'd rather he talked to June.

The first few questions are straightforward. He asks about Arbutus Academy and my acting credits, my feelings about landing the role of Iris and working with big stars like Brooklyn Cory and Etienne Quinn. I make sure I give every answer a positive spin.

"Plastic surgery?"

"None."

He raises an eyebrow in disbelief. "None," I repeat. Dad is totally against any kind of surgery. Mom is way more liberal, but for now she's backing Dad. That's fine by me. I hate needles. "Someday, maybe." Like when I'm forty.

"And your ethnicity is—?"

My unease grows. "I'm Canadian." I shut my eyes as Ellen dusts a fine coat of powder over my face. "Born and raised in Vancouver."

When I open my eyes, AJ is studying me, a puzzled look on his face.

"Vancouver, British Columbia?" I add. For sure he knows it.

"Yeah, got that." He taps his pen impatiently against his notepad. "But where did your parents come from? Originally, I mean."

The cape feels like it's choking me. I shift in the chair and run my finger around the neckline. Plus, it's making me hot. "My mother's Chinese and my father's Irish-German."

"Which one do you identify with?"

The million-dollar question. Either-or. Depends on who I'm with and what's going on. Or who's asking. But I can't tell him any of that, so I say, "I identify as Canadian."

"Not sexy enough," he says. "Have you been to China? To Ireland?"

"Yeah." I nod. "I've been to both. My mother and grandmother were born in China, so we go back every five years or so. And Dad's taken me to Ireland to see where his parents came from. He still has cousins there."

He writes something down. "Which one did you prefer?"

Sweat pools under my arms. He's leading me down a road I'm not willing to take. "They're both nice." I hesitate. "So's Canada."

He grimaces. "Canada is so white bread. At least Ireland is hearty brown."

Huh? What's with the bread thing? "White bread, brown bread, whatever. Anyway, I'm more like toasted sourdough." I give him a level glance, feigning a confidence I don't feel. "And we all know how good sourdough is."

He and Ellen laugh. After a few more questions—"Where are you staying?" "What do you think of LA?"—AJ heads for the door.

"There." Ellen wipes a tiny smear of lipstick from the corner of my mouth. "You're in paint." In paint. Made up for the cameras. She steps aside. "Lily, meet Iris."

I stare at my reflection. The camera washes everybody out, so I'm expecting tons of makeup. Ellen's gone heavy on the foundation and blush, yet my skin looks almost translucent. And she's given me cheekbones. "I look older."

"You're supposed to. Iris is twenty."

I tilt my head from side to side. I was worried about the false eyelashes, but she did a great job putting them on.

"Let me give you directions to the studio," she says, removing the cape. "You can't miss it."

* * *

Apparently, I can.

Panic rising, I stare down the narrow road at the silver trailers on either side of me. I turned right at the first intersection like Ellen told me to, and I've walked at least three minutes, but for sure I've gone the wrong way. There's no studio here.

There's nobody here. The place is quiet and deserted. And even though it's still early morning and only February, heat radiates up from the pavement. Gingerly, I blot my hairline. Ellen's makeup is starting to run. I need to get inside. Plus, I need to change!

When I pull out my cell to check the time, I practically hyperventilate. I'm due in the studio in exactly one minute.

This can't be happening. Anger bubbles up. If June had stayed...If Ellen had given me better directions. Maybe she did. Maybe I made the mistake. Tears sting my eyes. Maybe I was supposed to turn left, not right.

I force myself to take slow, deep breaths. Getting hysterical won't help. I need to retrace

my steps. Jog back to the intersection. Find somebody and get directions.

Behind me, a trailer door slams. Dizzy with
relief, I spin around. And I almost do a face-plant
in front of Etienne Quinn.

Six

"**W**hoa!" He rushes forward and grabs my arm, and all I can think is that his dimple is huge and he smells. In a good way. Like maple-sugar bacon. If there is such a thing. (If there isn't, somebody should get on it, because maple-sugar bacon is the best smell in the world.) "Steady there." He drops his hand.

I almost snatch it back, but that would show my creepy, stalkerish fangirl side, which might make him run. And I need directions. "I'm supposed to be on soundstage two in, like, three seconds, and Ellen in makeup told me to turn right only maybe I passed it or she made a mistake or...or something."

Or maybe I'm dreaming, and I'll wake up in rainy Vancouver instead of in front of the hottest guy I have ever smelled. I stare into his denim-colored eyes. He's wearing eyeliner? I look at his ugly green sweater. He's dressed like a dork?

It's makeup, you fool. A costume. This is a movie set, remember? You are an actress, *not a crazed fangirl.* I take a breath. "So now I'm late, plus I need to get into Iris's costume and—"

"You must be Lily."

Etienne Quinn knows my name? Face flames. Actress disappears. Crazed fangirl returns. "Yes, I—"

"You can change in your trailer."

OMG. His French accent is doing crazy things to my brain cells. "Trailer?"

He points to the unit just down from the one he stepped out of. "Number six. It was Naomi's. Now yours."

Nobody told me. But trailers on movie shoots are like flies at picnics. They're everywhere. I should have known. "Nobody gave me a key," I bluff, "so I thought I'd change on set."

"First day they leave the key inside." He pulls a cell phone from his pocket. "I'll tell them we'll be late."

We'll be late. He's going to wait. I bolt inside, vaguely registering two pink loveseats and a tiny kitchen with a microwave and small bar fridge. The key is propped against some pink roses and white daisies. *Welcome, Lily,* the card says. *Nic.*

OMG. Flowers. For me.

In the bathroom (massive, with a large vanity and changing area), I whip off my jeans and sweater and throw on the beige skirt, peach top and clunky black shoes. I check myself in the mirror. Eww. Gross.

Outside, Etienne is pacing. At least he looks like a loser too. I swallow. Except in a totally hot, non-loserish, movie-star kind of way. Wide shoulders. Narrow hips. Great butt. I stifle a snort of laughter. Too bad his jeans are so Value Village.

We start to walk. "Nic had an unexpected conference call, so he's pushed the start back half an hour."

"Great." *Great?* Man, I sound lame. I can't help it. I'm walking down the road beside Etienne Quinn, who smells like maple-sugar bacon. Who won an Emmy two years ago. Who dated

Brooklyn Cory even though she's practically old enough to be his mother.

He shoots me the famous Etienne look—a flick of too-blue eyes, a barely there smile, the flash of a dimple. Sexy flirt meets little boy lost. "So you're my love interest."

My throat constricts. Amazing I can still breathe. "Your guitar is your love interest, remember?"

He gives me a full-on grin this time. "I don't kiss my guitar."

OMG. He is such a flirt. Digging deep, I channel the always (unlike me) calm Iris. "You don't kiss me either."

"But I try to."

I look away. Yeah, he does. During a scene we shoot on location outside the library. Thankfully, I'm spared the need to answer because we reach the intersection. "So which way was I supposed to go?"

"Left, not right." We cross the street, passing a group of people dressed like space aliens. "Ellen's dyslexic."

Soundstage two is a cavernous space with massive ceilings crisscrossed with lights,

HOT NEW THING

ladders and support beams. The cameras and dollies have been pushed aside to make room for three long tables set up to form a giant U. Against the wall is a table with coffee, muffins, fruit and juice.

"Would you like something?"

"No, thanks, I'm good."

"I'll see you in a minute." He heads for the coffee.

You belong here, I remind myself as I step gingerly over the floor cables and head for a seat. *You're cast.*

My stomach flip-flops when I spot the placard spelling out my name—*Lily O'Neal/Iris.* Oh man! It's practically in the center of the U. I slide into my seat, open my script and hide behind it. This still feels like a dream. After a few minutes, a man wearing chef's whites slides into the chair beside me. "Hi, I'm John Samuel."

John Samuel. Mom went all giggly when she found out he plays my boss in the movie. Apparently, once he was hot like Etienne. Now he has wrinkles. And smile lines. He looks like a dad. "I'm Lily O'Neal."

"Pleased to meet you, Lily O'Neal."

The chairs soon fill up. Etienne sits beside me. Brooklyn is next to him. A dozen people obviously playing supporting roles fill the remaining seats nearby.

Nic welcomes us, spends a few minutes going over the shooting schedule and introduces the crew. Then he does a quick recap of the movie's premise.

"*Mom's Café* is about love and human potential," he says. "It's about ordinary people forced out of the rut of daily life by an unusual woman who shows up at the café in the fictional town of Harwood, Minnesota, and seems to know everything about them."

That woman would be me.

"We have Bill, the owner and chef." Beside me, John raises his hand. My character is supposed to help Bill find the courage to love again.

"His head waitress and love interest, Kim." Brooklyn gives the group a dainty wave. Kim's an alcoholic riddled with guilt. I remember Brooklyn's puffy, bloodshot eyes. Well cast.

"And Kim's brother, Michael." Etienne nods to the crowd. "Iris helps Michael conquer his self-doubt and pick up his guitar again when all he wants to do is get into her pants." I sneak a look at his crazy dimple. Those lips. My pulse quickens. Good thing the writers made Iris so pure. I couldn't kiss Etienne in private, never mind in front of a crowd.

"All three are trapped by routine and negativity," Nic continues. "Consequently, their lives are going nowhere." He looks at me. "Until Iris"—shyly I raise my hand—"shows up looking for work and is able to see beyond the lies these people have told themselves."

Nic quickly outlines the character arcs for Bill, Kim and Michael. I don't have a character arc. I disappear from Harwood, Minnesota, as suddenly and mysteriously as I arrive. After Nic introduces the secondary characters and answers questions, we start to read.

I first appear in the movie at the ten-minute mark. You'd think I could sit back and relax while the others read, but I can't. Not with my heart trampolining in my chest. I listen as Etienne goes from sexy French flirt to all-American boy as soon as he opens his mouth. John and Brooklyn are smooth and nuanced. By the time I deliver my first line, I am so panicked I can hardly talk.

"I saw your Help Wanted sign out front,"
I say. "I'm here about the job."

Beside me, John/Bill booms, "Have you
worked in a restaurant before?"

"I—"

Nic interrupts me. "Give me that last line
again, Iris. Only louder."

I suck in a quivery breath. Louder? I was
loud. Except the studio gobbles up sound, and
I've underestimated how much I need to project.
The mark of a total amateur. Pulling on my
training and my last scrap of confidence, I deliver
the line again. And nail it.

But it takes a few minutes before my breath
slows and I no longer feel a sharp jolt of fear
every time I open my mouth. When Nic calls
the lunch break, I'm exhausted. I've studied
for years, but no acting class, no movie of the
week, no commercial, has prepared me for how
hard this is.

"We're going out for lunch," Etienne says as
we push back our chairs. "We can't leave once
shooting starts. Want to come?"

Yes, no, I don't know. I'm unnerved, as if I've
taken a wrong step somewhere and can't find

my footing. I need to regroup. Alone. "Sorry, I can't make it. I—uh—" What? "I have this school assignment and—"

Confusion clouds his blue eyes. "School?"

Oh god, oh god, he probably thinks I'm twelve or something. "Final year," I lie. Maybe he'll think it's college. I check my watch. "And I need to text my instructor." *Liar.*

"School can wait."

I tilt my head and channel the cool, mystical Iris. "No, it can't."

He gives me *the look* and leans in close. I start to salivate over that yummy maple-sugar bacon smell. "Darlin', you and I need to talk."

It's a line from the movie, so I feed my lines back to him. "You're right. We do. About your guitar playing." But when I step sideways and almost fall over my chair, it totally blows the joke.

He laughs. "Go ahead and stay in character," he says, breaking from the script and going back to his French accent. "It doesn't matter to me whether you're Lily or Iris." He winks. "I could show either one of them a good time."

Seven

Mom to Lily: Too tired to Skype? Are you sick?
Lily to Mr. Basi: I need more time.
June to Lily: What, you're in a bakery now?

"**E**tienne Quinn was totally coming on to you," Claire screeches, and I pull the cell away from my ear. "Why aren't you more excited?"

"I *am* excited. I'm not dead, you know." I finish the last of my pasta. "But I'm not stupid, either."

"What do you mean?"

I put my plate down and flick on the light beside the bed. It's already dark. I didn't get home until after seven. "Etienne's like that with all the girls. It didn't mean anything. And I can't afford to get distracted. A million people would kill to be in my position."

Silence. Claire would kill to be in my position. She's been pretty clear about that. Or she was after I told her that if the situation were reversed and Nic Mills had picked her instead of me, I would have been totally jealous. It was like I'd given her permission to open up about feeling envious. I'm glad we talked about it. I wouldn't want this film to destroy our friendship.

"I'm on the brink of the career I've always wanted," I add. "I can't let anything get in my way." My gaze lands on my homework. Not even math.

"Etienne Quinn isn't just anything."

Yes, but..."Come on, Claire. Would you rather make out with Etienne or be a famous actress?"

More silence. Like she needs to think about it?

"Tough call," she finally says. And then she laughs.

I tell her about the rest of my day, how we spent the afternoon walking through the first few scenes, blocking out camera angles, checking lights. How the schedule is totally messed up because of Naomi's accident. How there's almost no time for rehearsals now and how tomorrow we start shooting. After promising on my life to keep her informed of all things Etienne, we say goodbye.

A few minutes later, when I take my dirty dishes to the kitchen, Aunt Joanne pops out of the family room.

"Did you get enough to eat?" She inclines her head politely, and her straight black hair—just like Sam's—swings with the movement.

"Yes, thanks." I consider joining her in front of the TV, but I have my script to read and my math to do and an early-morning call (and, anyway, she hasn't invited me), so I don't.

* * *

Tuesday morning when the car arrives, June's not there. Some chaperone. My parents would be choked if they knew she was mostly working for other clients instead of keeping an eye on me. I don't care—not really—but I do care about last night's weird text. I want to know what she meant. I texted her back, but she didn't answer.

When I get to my trailer, my call sheet is waiting and so is my costume. Thank goodness! I'm in the bathroom doing up my skirt when the front door bangs open.

"Lily!" June hollers. "What were you thinking?"

I hurry into the front room. June is standing beside the pink loveseat, bristling with anger. She waves a piece of paper in the air. "There were a million other things you could have said."

"What are you talking about?"

She glares at me. "You had to compare yourself to a piece of bread?"

Bread. Bakery. My mouth turns dry. Oh no. "That wasn't for the news release. That was a private joke."

"Nothing's private to a publicist," she snaps.

I bite back a snarky reply. This wouldn't have happened if she'd been doing her job. "He was on deadline and he left you a message, but you didn't call him back." Her gaze slides away. "He needed the information right away. I did the best I could."

She looks at me again, resignation and disappointment etched into her perma-tanned face. "Well, your best wasn't good enough." She shoves the paper at me. "Look."

Due to injury, Naomi Braithwaite has withdrawn from her role as Iris in Nic Mills' production of Mom's Café. Mr. Mills is pleased to announce that Lily O'Neal will be taking her place.

Ms. O'Neal has a long history of acting credits after years of study at the prestigious Arbutus Academy in Vancouver, Canada.

A true hapa with a Chinese mother and an Irish father, Ms. O'Neal prefers not to identify with any one culture, saying, "In the bakery of life, I'm like toasted sourdough."

While wishing Ms. Braithwaite the best in her recovery, Mr. Mills is delighted to work with Ms. O'Neal.

I look up. "I didn't say 'bakery of life.' He made that up."

"That's what PR people do," June wails. "Only it's up to us to ensure the stories they make up paint you in the best possible light. He should have run it by me first. Honestly, I—"

"And my father is Irish-German and—"

"German doesn't sell in Hollywood," June interrupts. "It's too close to Austria—Schwarzenegger ruined that for everybody."

I don't care about the Terminator. "And doesn't *hapa* mean half Hawaiian?"

"It's anybody who's mixed-race Asian American." She snatches the release from my hands.

"But I'm not Ameri—"

"And hapa sells well in Hollywood." She taps her watch. "Don't you have to go?"

I grab my shoes. She's right. I'm due in makeup in three minutes.

"This is Hollywood," June reminds me as we walk out the door. "This is the big time. Everything you say and do is fodder for the press. And for overworked publicists who want a fresh spin for everything. You'll be watched constantly, Lily. Never forget that."

* * *

June's words echo in my head as I walk into the studio. *This is the big time. You'll be watched constantly.*

As I stare at the crew crowding the set, I feel self-conscious. Did other people see the news release? Do they think I'm dumb too? To my relief, nobody pays any attention to me. Everyone is focused on the job at hand.

Overnight, *Mom's Café* has taken over sound-stage two. There's the front of the café with its sit-down counter and cash register. There's the kitchen with its industrial stove, walk-in refrigerator and prep area. My heart flip-flops. And there's the funky front entrance where I first appear on camera.

I spot John and Brooklyn in the kitchen, walking through a scene with Nic. Etienne is slouched in a black director's chair, studying his lines.

A chubby guy wearing a headset and a too-tight plaid shirt hurries over. "Oh, Lily, hi." His name tag reads *G. Rangler. Script Supervisor.* "We've made changes to your scene." He hands me some sheets with my name scrawled at the top. "I've emailed you a copy and printed them out as well. Your changes are in blue."

A chill shoots through me. I was up half the night running lines with my iPad. Now I have to learn new ones? I skim the pages. And there are a lot of them.

Oh crap.

You can do this. You're a pro. You've done improv.

The first day passes in a blur as everyone struggles with the changes and Nic's many demands. At lunchtime, I hide in my trailer, telling everybody I have homework to do. Thank goodness I stuffed my iPad into my bag when I left Uncle Mike's. I pull up the rehearsal app, download the email with the script changes, import the new dialogue and get to work learning my new lines. Luckily, my first scene is with John, who is easy to work with even if he keeps missing his mark when he walks into the scene. It's up and down for the rest of the afternoon, and by the time we finish for the night, everybody's worn out and cranky.

* * *

Wednesday, I do my first scene with Brooklyn. Though we've blocked our moves and spent an hour rehearsing before the cameras roll, Brooklyn constantly changes things, forcing me to improvise. Once, she feeds me the wrong line. When I hesitate and Nic calls, "Cut," Brooklyn's eyes flash *Gotcha.*

63

In spite of my flubs, Nic is complimentary. "Great blend of detachment and concern," he tells me when we stop for lunch. He's wearing his usual denim ballcap and a brilliant fuchsia Hawaiian shirt. "You're hitting all the right notes, Lily."

Brooklyn shoots me a venomous look as she leads Nic away. "What about me?" I hear her ask. "Am I hitting the right notes?"

After lunch, Brooklyn's nastiness gets worse. So does my performance. Not only do I flub my lines, but I forget all about continuity. The script supervisor jumps all over me when I pick up a coffee cup with my left hand and then, when we reshoot the scene, forget and pick it up with my right. I flick my hair a couple of times when I'm not supposed to as well. Nic continues to encourage me, but his impatience shows. By the time the car drops me at Uncle Mike's later that night, I'm exhausted. All I want to do is eat and crash. But tomorrow I shoot my first scene with Etienne, and I want to run my lines again. Plus, I still have math to do.

I drop my stuff in the bedroom and head for the kitchen. When I reach the doorway, I see Samantha and Uncle Mike having an argument.

I don't know what they're saying—they're speaking Mandarin—but Samantha's hands are clenched at her side, and Uncle Mike's tone is clipped.

Awkward. I clear my throat and wait a few seconds before removing a pasta dinner from the freezer and putting it in the microwave.

They continue to talk, though my uncle's voice is calmer. It's only when he calls my name that I realize he's talking to me.

I turn to face them. "I'm sorry. I don't speak Mandarin."

He immediately switches to English. "Will that be enough dinner for you?" He doesn't look like Mom, but I see a little of Grandma in his kind brown eyes.

"Yes, thanks. Sorry I was late and missed dinner again."

"Don't apologize. We understand you have a job to do." He gives me a polite smile, the kind you give to strangers who hold the door open at the mall. "Feel free to use our home as you would your own."

Samantha rolls her eyes.

"Thanks." The microwave beeps. I remove my food, gather cutlery from the drawer and leave.

The TV is on in the family room. The warm, comforting sound of the laugh track reminds me of home. I know I need to work on tomorrow's scene—and tackle my math—but I miss my parents, and I miss Claire. I could use the reassurance of a familiar face. Some company while I eat.

But then I hear Samantha say, "I don't know why you spoke Mandarin to her. She's white, not Asian."

My foot catches on the carpet, and I almost stumble. Story of my life. My Asian cousins say I'm white, and my white cousins say I'm Asian. Neither side claims me as their own. When I reach the family room, I keep on going. I don't fit. And I don't need another reminder.

Eight

On Thursday I arrange for the driver to drop me at the studio forty minutes early so I can have some quiet time alone in my trailer before we start shooting. I'm anxious about my first scene with Etienne. My worry is unfounded. Etienne is a generous actor, not stealing the scene from me but throwing himself into his role and helping me look good in the process. The energy between us is amazing, and I manage to channel the coolly mysterious Iris without missing a beat. At lunchtime, John drops a fatherly arm across my shoulders. "No hiding in your trailer doing homework today." He leads me to the food table. "You're eating with us." As I sit with the group and listen to them talk about the shoot, I start to relax. This is my tribe. I get these people. Even better, they get me. My confidence grows. I have a future in this industry—I know I do.

* * *

On Friday everything falls apart.

"You look tired," Ellen says when I get to makeup that morning. She blends extra concealer under my eyes. "You out partying last night?"

I laugh. "I wish." Instead, I stayed up way too late finishing my math. Or trying to. I emailed everything off this morning, but I know some of the answers are wrong.

When I get to the studio, dozens of people are bustling around, moving cameras and adjusting lights. Extras watch the activity with barely concealed excitement. "Morning, Lily," says a grip as I head to the food table. "How're you doing today?"

I smile back. I'm no longer a stranger. I've truly found my place. "Good, thanks."

Then I see a familiar plaid shirt. It's George Rangler, holding an armload of papers. My heart sinks. Oh no. Not again. "Nic says to take fifteen and read through the changes." He presses the sheets into my hand.

As I read through my new lines, a headache starts at the base of my skull. This is a busy scene. It's the first time Etienne, John, Brooklyn and I are in a scene together. Plus, there's supporting cast. One slip and the whole thing falls apart.

We start shooting late, mostly because Nic and the cinematographer decide to change camera angles, which means lighting has to be changed too. This puts Nic in a bad mood. He stops John repeatedly, unhappy with the inflection in his voice as he delivers his new lines to Brooklyn. Then continuity jumps on Brooklyn for changing her angles when she pours coffee for a customer. By the time it's sorted out, my headache is so bad I'm almost nauseous. And when my turn comes, I keep blowing my lines.

"Cut!" Nic tugs on his ballcap and bolts from his chair.

Oh crap. That's ten times I've messed up.

"Oh my god," Brooklyn mutters. She turns to John and rolls her eyes.

I'm tired, achy and nervous. It's a terrible combination, and it's affecting my performance.

"This is a pivotal scene," Nic says when he reaches us. "Iris, you're sharing an insight about a regular." He gestures to the woman sitting on the stool pretending to nurse a coffee. "It's important that you get this scene right. Let's take it from the top."

Everybody groans.

"From the top," Nic insists, looking at me. "This time I want you to feed Brooklyn only one line. 'Sometimes you know things about people.' Just that line. Can you do that?"

Oh man. He's treating me like a total newbie. My humiliation is complete. I nod.

"You get that line right and we'll try a take with the whole thing. If it doesn't work, we'll do some creative editing."

Sometimes you know things about people, I repeat silently as we assume our positions. I glance at Brooklyn. She's whispering to John and smirking. Sometimes you do know things about people. And right now, I know Brooklyn loves the fact that I'm struggling.

"Quiet on the set," the first AD calls. "Roll sound."

The camera assistant steps forward. "*Mom's Café*, scene eleven. Take thirty." He drops the clapboard.

"Rolling," Nic shouts.

John walks out of the kitchen, delivers his line to Brooklyn. She pours coffee for the customer and exchanges a few words with her. Then I walk into the scene, stop on my mark, look Brooklyn in the eye and say, "Sometimes you know things about people." And for some crazy reason, the rest of my lines just flow, almost like someone has turned a key and unlocked them.

Nic keeps rolling. We're good for another minute or so, until Etienne blows a line to me. We do a retake. Etienne and I get through our exchange, but I flub a line to John.

"Cut!" Nic hollers. "Take a break."

My headache stabs like nails behind my eyes. I'm miserable. I wish I could hide in my trailer. Instead, I go to the set bathroom, where I run cold water over a paper towel and blot the back of my neck. When I hear the door open, I hurry into the last stall. I need privacy. I need this pain to go away.

"Lily is pathetic." It's Brooklyn, talking to someone. "She couldn't deliver a line if her life depended on it."

My headache throbs. I'm not pathetic. Nic sees something in me. And he's good at picking winners.

"She's not that bad." I recognize the voice. It's an assistant producer named Marnie.

Brooklyn counters. "She is *so* that bad. She looks odd too. Just not relatable."

I grit my teeth. *Relatable.* The Hollywood description for the girl-next-door look. So what? Looking different got me to Hollywood. I keep myself still as they use the washroom. I pray they don't notice my feet underneath the stall door.

"She needs to stop playing actress and go home to Mama," Brooklyn adds a few minutes later when they're washing their hands. "Either that or get a boob job. Have you seen that body?"

Whoa. White-hot fury roars through me.

"Nic needed someone unique," Marnie says. "Iris is a one-of-a-kind role."

Brooklyn snorts. "Yeah, so one of a kind it'll probably be Lily's first and last movie."

That's not fair! When the bathroom door slams behind them, I rush from the stall and bolt out of the bathroom. I want to grab them, shake them, tell them they aren't being nice. But all I can do is watch them walk away laughing. I'm no one-shot wonder. I stare at Brooklyn's butt. And so what if I'm skinny? At least I don't look like the Pillsbury Doughboy.

Infuriated and more determined than ever to prove myself, I manage to get through the rest of the day. By the time we finish, it's close to nine and everyone is tense, irritable and ready for the weekend.

It's dark as Etienne and I make our way back to the trailers. Recessed spotlights turn the squat Pallas-Mills buildings yellow-gold. A light breeze rustles the papery fronds of a palm tree. I smell cigarettes. Someone, somewhere, is smoking.

"What are you doing this weekend?"

A tiny thrill races up my spine. Etienne Quinn is asking me what I'm doing this weekend. Who would've guessed?

"I'm busy."

He slides me that sideways look. "Too busy to go out?"

I practically swallow my tongue. With him? For real? *Earth to Lily: You are imagining things.* "Yeah, too busy. I've got homework and..." I need to Skype with my parents. "And other stuff," I finish weakly.

Up ahead, Brooklyn and John share a laugh. I wonder if they're talking about me.

"You spend a lot of time doing homework," Etienne says.

"Yeah, well, what can I say? I'm a keener." And I'm lousy at math.

"I know this guy," Etienne says as we cross the road. "I could give you his number."

My clunky black shoes catch on a rock, and I almost stumble. Etienne is trying to set me up? With a guy I don't know? "I don't do blind dates."

He laughs. "Not that kind of guy. A brainiac. You hire him to do your homework for you."

"Seriously?" The question pops out before I can stop it. Naïve, June called me. Maybe she's right. "I mean, I know they're around, but..." I shrug. "I hadn't given it a lot of thought."

He stops in front of his trailer. "Where's your cell?"

"Inside."

He pulls a pen from his pocket, reaches for my hand and turns it palm side up. My knees go weak. "Here's my number." He starts to scribble.

My entire hand is on fire. I hold my breath. For a second, it's like I'm living in some kind of parallel universe. Something I've spun from my dreams. Los Angeles and this movie set. My role in *Mom's Café*. Etienne Quinn, who smells too good to be real.

"I've got his number somewhere at home. Call me if you want it." He winks, drops my hand and lopes up the three steps to his trailer. When the door slams behind him, I slam back to reality and give myself a mental shake.

This is not a parallel universe. It's not a dream. This is my life. I watch Brooklyn walk up the steps to her trailer. A life I've worked long and hard to create. I stick my tongue out at her fat, Pillsbury Doughboy ass. Take that, Brooklyn Cory.

Nine

Lily to Claire: It is _so_ his cell number.
Claire to Lily: It's not. Nobody that famous
writes their number on somebody's hand.
Did u try it?
Lily to Claire: I texted. It showed as unknown.
Claire to Lily: See!
Mom to Lily: We need to talk.

"**M**r. Basi is concerned, Lily—that's
why he contacted us." Mom's move-
ments are jerky with the Skype delay.
She's on our couch at home, sandwiched between
Dad and Grandma. I'm on Uncle Mike's sectional
with my iPad resting in the V of my crossed legs.
"And we're concerned too."

I stifle a sigh. Twelve hundred miles from home, and I still feel guilty. Behind them, I see the view from our living room window. The street's wet. A woman in Gore-Tex is walking down the sidewalk, holding a yellow umbrella. My throat swells. I miss the rain. It's so hot and dry here that my hair snaps when I brush it.

"Over half your answers were wrong," Dad adds.

Three quarters of them, actually. Basi emailed me too. "He's sending some makeup assignments. I'll do better next time. Can you ask the bank to raise my daily-withdrawal limit?"

"Why?"

Because I'm hiring that brainiac guy Etienne mentioned. If I can ever get the number. Etienne still hasn't answered my text message. "I want to go shopping," I bluff. "There are some great stores here."

"When will you have time to shop?" Mom asks.

"They have to give me a day off once in a while."

"Forget shopping!" Dad says. "We want you to get an education."

I want an education too, but I also want to be an actress, and right now that's more important.

"How 'bout I show you the rest of the house?" I jump up and head for the kitchen. "You need to see the deck."

Grandma starts chattering in Mandarin; I am saved.

Sunday, I'm supposed to meet June for lunch. The cab drops me off early, so I check out True Religion at Beverly Center, followed by H&M a few blocks away. The breeze smells of ocean and exhaust as I wander down West Third, staring into the shop windows and checking out the people cruising by. After a while, the women all look the same: big shoes + big sunglasses + big hair extensions = smaller-looking butt. I should send a memo to Brooklyn.

I get to Joan's on Third before June and am waiting for a table when she texts me. Something's come up. Must cancel.

Typical. She's probably meeting with one of her other clients. I step out of line.

See U next week, she adds. AJ says U need to be more visible. Don't hide in trailer so much.

It turns out that won't be hard.

* * *

When I get to the studio on Monday, Nic announces that we'll be filming on location in Santa Paula on Friday. AJ will be happy. But my anxiety skyrockets. That means shooting the scene where Etienne tries to kiss me.

At least I don't have to worry about math. At lunch, Etienne gives me the phone number for Mr. Brainiac (aka Sean somebody-or-other). "Sorry I didn't get it to you on the weekend." His blue eyes gleam. "Now you'll have more time to spend with me, yes?"

Etienne would flirt with an empty soda can. I shrug. "I'll see."

He just laughs.

I email everything to the brainiac on Monday night, relieved that I can concentrate solely on the shoot. And I throw myself into the role of Iris with everything I've got.

"My god, that was brilliant, Lily," Nic tells me with a broad smile as we wrap up Thursday. "I loved how you ad-libbed that line about forgiveness being something you cultivate."

"Thanks."

Some say the ability to act is a gift, but to me it's about logic. Roles are defined. I know going in what I'm supposed to portray. It's easier than life, where everyone expects me to be something different and I can never find my footing.

* * *

On Friday the car picks me up at 6:30 AM for the hour-long drive north to Santa Paula. It's an old-fashioned town with brick buildings, flower boxes and angled street parking. A perfect stand-in for small-town Minnesota.

As the driver coasts down Main Street, I spot the crew outside what's obviously the *Mom's Café* set. A sidewalk sign with the familiar red-and-yellow café logo is positioned beside a doorway, probably a functional restaurant they've rented for the shoot. Across the street is a temporary sign for the Lucky Tavern, where I rescue a drunken Brooklyn and take her home. I gnaw on a hangnail. Soon after that scene comes my "don't kiss me" scene with Etienne. With luck, we won't get to it until next week.

My luck sucks. I'm in makeup when the first AD shows up with my call sheet to tell me we're shooting that scene first.

"We didn't consider the angle of the morning sun," he explains as he walks me down the block to the historic Limoneira building. "So we're shooting out of sequence." Doing scenes out of sequence happens often on shoots, so I'm not surprised. But I am disappointed.

As we turn the corner to the set, my shoulder blades tighten. Hundreds of spectators are clustered in front of the beautiful Spanish-style structure, which is standing in as the Harwood Library. Hundreds. Plus, there's a tent for the sound guys. Extra camera and boom operators. And lights. So many lights.

"Is that somebody?" asks a woman in a jean jacket as I walk toward Etienne and Nic. "She's in costume and all made up."

"She's nobody," her friend says. They peer behind me to see who else is coming.

Normally, the comment would make me smile. But today I'm uneasy. Seeing a set in the middle of the street, with birds flying around and cars driving past, seems so unreal. Plus, Etienne is going to try to kiss me.

It's just acting, I remind myself when I reach them. It'll be fine.

Except shooting outside is so not easy.

"Cut!" Nic shouts ninety minutes later when a lawn mower starts up and drowns out my words. A collective groan rises. First it was wind. Then traffic. Now this.

Somebody is dispatched to find the offending lawn cutter. Ellen rushes forward, her makeup belt slung around her waist, to powder my nose. Nic wanders over to remind us of the specifics of the scene.

"Remember, Iris wants Michael to accept his musical talent." He turns to Etienne. "And Michael wants to mess around and not think about his gift."

Nic goes back to his chair. The lawn mower stops. Etienne and I assume our places on the stairs.

"Quiet on the set," the first AD calls. The crowd grows silent. "Roll sound."

The camera assistant steps forward. "*Mom's Café*, scene twenty-nine, take thirteen." He drops the clapboard.

Lucky thirteen. I lean against the arch for support. Lucky, lucky thirteen.

"Rolling!" Nic shouts.

I clutch the library books I've supposedly checked out and look up at Etienne/Michael. "You're good, Michael."

He grins. "You have no idea how good I am." He walks down a step and puts his arm on the wall beside me. "But we could change that."

I gaze up, cool and composed. "I'm talking about your guitar playing."

"I'm not." There's a flash in his blue eyes. "Come home with me, Iris. You know you want to." Slowly, he lowers his head to mine.

My heart stutters. For a millisecond, art blurs with life and I'm plain old Lily O'Neal standing in front of Etienne Quinn and I think, What the hell, but then my training kicks in. "No." I slide out from under his arm. "I want you to go home and get your guitar. A gift like yours shouldn't be wasted."

I walk down the last four stairs. When I reach the yellow mark past the garden beds, Nic yells, "Cut." Seconds later, he adds, "That's a wrap."

Whew.

"Lunch break," the second AD hollers. "See everybody at two."

Etienne heads toward me. A cluster of girls behind the ropes shrieks, "Etienne! Over here!"

"Your fan club is waiting," I say when he reaches me. I'm so relieved the scene is over, I am actually trembling.

"Don't make me face them alone." His French accent is back.

"What? You're shy now?"

"No, I am smart. The last time I faced a crowd this big, some woman tore the shirt off my back."

I snicker and look at his ugly striped shirt. "I don't think you need to worry."

Before I can stop him, he grabs my hand and steers me to the ropes.

"Etienne! Sign this!" Papers and pens jab the air.

"Here, do mine."

"You too!" The lady in the jean jacket shoves a scrap of paper at me. "You practically kissed him."

Wait till I tell Claire, I think as I sign and sign and sign. She will die.

"Will you be at the Copper Awards?" someone shouts as we turn to go.

The Coppers are up there with the Golden Globes. A red-carpet night designed to show-case the best in social media. Hollywood turns out big time.

"Of course." Etienne drops an arm across my shoulders. "Lily and I will both be there."

My mouth gapes. "We will?"

"Absolutely. Naomi was supposed to be my date, but she's in a cast. You're it, Lily." He winks. "You can't hide this time."

Ten

Lily to Mom: FedEx GAP dress to Uncle Mike's.
ASAP.

Lily to Claire: I'm going to the Coppers with E.
PLUS I signed autographs.

Mr. Basi to Lily: Good work. One last assignment
attached.

Sean Tribley to Lily: Yes, I can do a science
paper. U owe me $180 so far.

The crowd roars as we step out of the limousine at the Copper Awards just over a week later. "Etienne! Over here!!"

Camera flashes temporarily blind me. When they clear, I see the massive Shrine Auditorium with its yellow-domed turrets...a mile-long swath of cherry-red carpet. My heart stutters. There are hundreds of screaming fans. Smiling reporters. Shimmering celebrities.

"Hold my hand," Etienne murmurs when I hesitate. I'm wearing a calf-length blue-grey dress with floaty sleeves and high black stilettos. (GAP won't cut it, Ellen said. She'd called up a designer friend and had them send three dresses and a couple of pairs of shoes to the studio for me to try. It was the best non-shopping trip of my life.) Etienne is wearing a black suit! And cologne. He smells like *musky* maple-sugar bacon. Total yum.

I take his hand, though I'm not nervous. All we have to do is watch the awards and smile a lot. And talk to reporters, which Etienne does seconds after we hit the red carpet.

As he talks, I scan the people nearby. And I turn cold with shock. There's Channing Tatum. Only a few feet away. Close enough to touch. Oh my god.

"Yes," Etienne says, "Lily is my co-star." I snap back to attention.

The next few minutes are a fast-moving blur of famous faces—Ellen! Sophia Grace and Rosie! Anne Hathaway!—and reporters. It's so unreal, I have to remind myself to breathe.

"Steve!" a reporter yells.

Etienne's hold on my hand tightens. "Keep moving."

"Steve Quinn. Over here!"

Anger flashes in his eyes, but his smile never falters. "It's Etienne, you prick," he mutters. Without breaking stride, he spins me to the other side of the red carpet.

"What was that about?"

"Nothing."

It's definitely something. A red flush is creeping up the back of his neck.

"Some people are just bastards," he whispers when he sees me staring. "No matter how good a job you do, you're never enough."

His French accent is noticeable, and I think maybe he's gotten his words mixed up. "*It's* never enough, you mean?"

"No." He shakes his head. "*You're* never enough."

And then we're inside. My breath stops when I see the amazing ceiling that looks like the inside of a sheik's tent, the massive chandelier with colored bulbs, the rows and rows of red velvet seats.

Steve Martin is MC. His comments as he hands out the awards for the best in social media have everybody howling. By intermission, my stomach hurts from laughing.

"Champagne?" Etienne asks as we stand and stretch.

A ripple of unease skitters down my spine. Mom would kill me. But tonight is special. "Sure." One glass won't hurt.

He heads for the bar, and I get in line for the bathroom. As I'm walking back to my seat, a dark-haired woman in a tight black column dress stops me. She reminds me of a panther.

"Lily O'Neal, I'm so pleased to meet you." She has flawless skin and large, almond-shaped eyes. "I'm sorry. You probably don't know who I am." Her red lips curve into a smile. "Damarais Hill. I saw you on location last week in Santa Paula."

We shot there for six days. By the end, people were actually asking me for my autograph. Calling out my name when I walked by. I lost track of how many people I talked to.

"Pleased to meet you," I say.

She pulls a card from her black clutch. "I'm the Hill in the Trainer and Hill Agency."

The bottom drops out of my stomach. Trainer and Hill is one of the biggest talent agencies in Hollywood. "Of course."

"I understand you're represented by a Vancouver firm, but have you considered going with an agency in Los Angeles?" She presses her card into my palm. "If you want to talk, give me a call. We can do wonderful things for you."

Between Damarais Hill and the champagne, I'm giddy and I don't want the night to end. So when Etienne invites me to a party in Laurel Canyon, I say yes. But by the time the limo drops us in front of an ivy-covered yellow mansion, I'm having second thoughts.

"We shouldn't stay long," I say as we follow the sound of laughter past garden beds filled with white flowers.

"Why not? I'm off tomorrow and you have a late call." He nods at a burly bald guy guarding a side gate. "Hey, Sam."

The man nods and swings the gate open.

The back of the mansion is as spectacular as the front. Massive kidney-shaped pool. Swim-up bar. Two tiered patios leading to a light-filled house. I almost trip when I see a woman swimming naked in the pool. "Careful." Etienne takes my arm. "The tiles are slippery."

Two levels up is another bar, plus food tables and a dance floor. "I need the bathroom," Etienne says. "You okay for a minute?"

At least everyone here is dressed. "Sure. Meet me by the food."

There's quite a spread. Oysters on the half shell. Cracked crab claws. Pearls of black caviar on potato skins. Sushi. Tiny crudités. A selection of cheeses. My mouth starts to water. Little lamb meatballs. And I am starving.

I scarf down a meatball, a cherry tomato stuffed with shrimp, and a few squares of cheese. Now I'm thirsty, but the bar is crowded so I check out the three punch bowls instead. Citrus-rum, tropical bourbon or iced fruit. Iced fruit should be safe. I ladle some into a cup and take a sip. It's too sweet, but at least it's booze-free. I fill my cup and turn to the sushi. I'm about to pick up a piece of California roll when a horsey-looking woman wearing gold palazzo pants and a cream wrap comes up beside me. "Hello, Lily. It's nice to see you again."

At least I remember her. She's Pat Landsberg, a producer Nic introduced me to on set last week.

"Hello!" I gulp down some punch. I'm relieved to see a familiar (but not famous) face.

"My husband and I are sitting over there." She points to a short, stout man loaded with bling. "Why don't you fill up your cup and join us?"

Pat's husband, Richard, quickly puts me at ease, asking about my experience and how I'm finding the role of Iris and making sure I never run out of punch. He offers to get me something to eat at one point, but I say no. With my luck, I'd probably drop a chunk of sushi down my dress or something. When Etienne walks by and gives me a questioning look, I give him a thumbs-up. A few minutes later, when Richard says they're casting for an upcoming movie and asks if I'd consider taking on a part, I almost choke on my drink. "Of course," I say.

Pat stands. "There are a few people Rich and I would like you to meet."

When I stand, the pool seems to tilt. I'm light-headed with excitement.

And my excitement builds. Pat and Richard escort me around the patio, introducing me to their friends and associates—more producers, another director. Business card after business card is pressed into my hand, along with cup after cup of punch. People can't do enough for me.

"She's a beautiful girl," someone says. "Like a china doll." The words drift by. I feel weirdly disconnected. Time and conversations are blurring; names are running together.

"I need to find Etienne. I need to go." My mouth feels thick, like I'm talking around a pair of socks.

"Tell your agent to call us as soon as possible so we can get this offer on the table." Pat hands me her card.

That makes six. I fumble with my clutch. Or is it seven? I've lost track. "I need the bathroom first."

"Of course. It's inside through the media room." She motions to the open patio door. "Turn right, go down the hall. You can't miss it."

There's a movie playing, but the images on the screen are blurred. "Somebody should fix that," I mumble, walking unsteadily down the hall. Inside the bathroom, the room starts to spin. I grab the vanity and stare at my reflection until the walls stop moving. I lean into the glass and stare at a tiny mole beside my mouth.

Oops. It's not a mole. It's a tiny piece of lamb. A lamb mole. I giggle. And everybody in the whole wide party world has seen it. My laughter deepens. Whatever. I brush it away.

A few minutes later, when I wander back to the media room, Etienne is waiting.

I collapse into a black recliner. My legs feel like I'm walking under water. "Hey, Mr. Maple-Sugar Bacon Man." I hesitate, grappling for a memory. "No. Wait. Mr. *Musky* Maple-Sugar Bacon Man." My eyes are so heavy, I swear I could sleep for a year.

Etienne crouches beside me. He's taken off his tie and loosened the top buttons on his shirt. "Are you okay?"

"'Course I'm okay." I gesture to the screen. "That's not okay though. That movie's out of focus."

He just watches me.

"What's wrong? Is my lamb mole back?" I giggle again.

He frowns. "Lamb mole?"

"Yeah, everybody saw it. But that's okay because everybody really, really likes me." I straighten. I trace the outline of his lips with the tip of my finger. "You like me too, right, Etienne?"

His blue eyes darken. "I—"

I cut him off. "Come home with me," I tease. It's like the movie, only backward. "You know you want to." I drop my hand to his shoulder and pull him close. And this time we really do kiss.

His mouth is warm, fruity and sharp. I could drown in his taste. I slide my arms around his neck and pull him closer. I really could.

He lifts his head and gently removes my hands from his neck. "Did you eat the sushi?"

"No. Yes. I can't remember." I struggle to think back.

"I hope not," Etienne says. "That was happy sushi. It was laced with pot."

"I didn't." Skepticism flashes across his face. "I didn't, didn't, didn't," I insist in a singsong voice. "But I did have a lamb meatball." I snicker. "That's where I got the lamb mole. And I drank lots and lots of iced fruit punch."

"Ah." He tugs me to my feet. "That explains it."

"Explains what?"

"You're drunk, Lily."

"No way. That was fruit punch. Fruit as in way-too-sweet fruit punch." I giggle again.

LAURA LANGSTON

"That was vodka fruit punch. It's sweetened for people who hate the taste of booze." He puts his arm around me and guides me to the door. "Come on. We need to sober you up. You're totally hammered."

Eleven

Lily to June: We need to talk. I've had offers!!!!!!!!!!!!!!
Claire to Lily: There's a picture of you and Etienne in the Vancouver Sun!!!!!
Dad to Lily: We have a problem, young lady.

"Don't do it again," June says as the driver coasts to a stop outside Uncle Mike's house the following night. I'm glad the day is over. I don't know how people work when they're hungover. I barely managed, even with my late call. And boy, did Ellen have to do a lot of magic in makeup to make me look human. "I covered for you this time, but I won't in the future."

Of course she covered for me. June's supposed to be chaperoning. If my parents found out she wasn't, they'd be furious with her.

Living room lights glow through the dark silhouette of the tree in the front yard. It's almost eleven, but somebody's still up. Oh, man. A headache pounds behind my eyes. This won't be good.

"Next time, text me if you're going somewhere after an event." The streetlight makes her perma-tanned face look like rough adobe. "At least Etienne finally answered your cell phone."

Yeah, at 2:00 AM as we were driving the streets of LA while he sobered me up with milky coffee and greasy French fries. By then, my aunt was frantic. How was I supposed to know she'd check on me before she went to bed? Apparently, she's done it before, but I've always been asleep.

"I told them you had my permission but you lost track of time."

She doesn't know about the punch, then. Etienne was smart enough not to mention it. "Thanks." I gesture to the business cards she's holding. "So you'll follow up with Richard and Pat? And the others?" Three producers mentioned specific roles. Two others wanted *to talk possibilities.*

"Yes, Lily. With everyone."

After confirming tomorrow's pickup time with the driver, I head for the front door, gingerly sliding my key into the lock. My aunt and uncle said very little last night, though they were obviously furious. They told me to go to bed, that we would discuss things when they were calmer. I know I need to apologize, and I will, but not tonight. Please, not tonight.

The door swings open. I see a pair of ugly striped socks, a faded gray sweat suit. Samantha. Her face impassive, she gestures to the living room. "They want to see you."

Crap. Aunt Joanne is curled into the corner of the couch, her dressing gown pulled tight. Uncle Mike is beside her, his hair sticking up at the back. Guilt twinges. They've dozed off waiting for me.

"We were worried last night," he says.

Worried enough to call my parents. I know. Mom and Dad reamed me out long distance first thing this morning. "I'm so sorry." I perch stiffly on the chair across from them. "I didn't mean to upset you."

My gaze lands on the newspaper lying on the coffee table. It's open to the picture of me and Etienne arriving at the party. Thank God we weren't photographed leaving.

"We want you to use our home as your own, but that means having enough respect to let us know when you'll be late," Uncle Mike says.

"We have certain expectations," Joanne adds. "Obviously, you do things differently in your house."

Not true, I want to say. My parents freaked too. But her stern frown stops me.

He clears his throat. "While you're here, you must tell us if you plan to come in after midnight."

"It may be a foreign concept," Joanne says, "but it's how we do things in our family."

Our family. Message received. I'm an outsider here.

"Of course." I get up, and my gaze falls on the newspaper again. I wasn't an outsider at the party. Everybody wanted to talk to me.

As I walk down the hall, Samantha pokes her head out of her room. "Was it worth it?"

Instead of judgment in her dark eyes, there's only curiosity. "Totally." The punch was a mistake, and one I won't repeat (pizza and sushi are to be avoided too, Etienne said last night), but I'm glad I went. "So totally."

A half smile flits across her face as she shuts the door.

I made some important connections last night. And connecting is the name of the game in Hollywood. It's a sign that I've arrived.

* * *

Tuesday morning, however, when I arrive at the studio and see Etienne standing by the coffee, the only thing I feel is a hot rush of embarrassment. I'm dreading this. I haven't seen him since I kissed him in the media room. And in the limo too. Shame worms through me.

Girls throw themselves at him all the time, Claire had told me when we talked Monday. For sure he's used to it.

Maybe, but I'm not most girls. Making my mark in Hollywood doesn't mean I should lower my standards. I take a deep breath and force myself to move. I need to get this over with.

"Morning, Lily," the AD says when I reach them.

"Morning."

Etienne looks over and smiles. I turn away, pour coffee, add way too much sugar. When the

AD leaves, I squelch my humiliation and turn around.

His dimple flashes as he gives me that classic Etienne look, the combination of sexy flirt and little boy lost. "Had any punch this morning?"

My face heats up a thousand degrees. He laughs.

"Look, I'm really sorry, okay? You probably have the totally wrong idea, but I don't normally act that way. It's not who I am, and I need you to know that."

"It's no big deal," he says as we wander over to the chairs. "It's not the first time."

Somehow that is not comforting. "I don't want it to get in the way of our"—our what? Friendship? Budding romance? Working relationship?—"our work on set," I finish weakly.

"It won't." We sit and watch John take his place on set for his first scene of the day with Brooklyn. "How did it go with your agent yesterday?"

"Good." I'm relieved he's changed the subject. "She promised to follow up on the offers right away."

"Keep on top of her," he says. "Nobody cares about your career as much as you. I learned that the hard way."

Early in his career, Etienne had a disastrous relationship with a business manager who insisted he be called Steven, the English translation of Etienne. The relationship ended publicly and badly. I found out last night when I googled *Steve "Etienne" Quinn.*

"You're on your way, Lily. Pat and Richard are top producers. Anything they touch is box-office gold."

* * *

On your way. Box-office gold. I remind myself of Etienne's comments over the next few days as I work on the film and wait for June to get back to me. On Wednesday, AJ asks me to do a phone interview with a reporter from the *Hollywood Slate.* Wary of being misquoted, I ask for the questions ahead of time, and the interview goes well. I text June about it and at the same time ask if she's been in touch with any of the producers. She doesn't reply. By Friday, I'm anxious. By Sunday, I'm mad. I don't need her holding my hand every minute, but she is supposed to be chaperoning me.

LAURA LANGSTON

On Monday morning, we finally connect by phone as I'm dressing in my trailer.

"Richard's role wasn't suitable for you," she says. I hear the sound of a coffee grinder in the background and someone shouting, "Tall dark to go."

I fasten my skirt and walk into the living area. "What do you mean, it wasn't suitable?" I wiggle into my black Iris shoes.

"Just that." The background sounds fade. "It was too mature. Too edgy."

I fall into the pink loveseat. "What about the other producers? What about their projects?"

"A level of sophistication...some violence... not comfortable..."

"You're cutting out!"

"...simply not the right roles for you...better for my other clients...recommending them instead."

"What?" Shocked, I stare at the weekly flower arrangement on the glass side table. The pretty yellow daisies and white freesias mock me with their cheerfulness. "You suggested other clients?"

"I have to do what's best for my clients, Lily." June's voice is full strength again, but I feel like

104

I'm under water. I am so stunned, her words sound garbled. "There will be other roles for you, dear. Don't worry."

Sound comes out of my mouth. Something mechanical. June starts to respond, but I cut her off. "I have to go." Jumping up, I hurry to the kitchen counter. "Someone's waiting for me."

I disconnect and pick up my purse. Someone *is* waiting for me. I flick the clasp and remove the only business card I didn't pass to June.

Damarais Hill. It's time I talked to her.

Twelve

Claire to Lily: Srsly??????? June turned them down?

Mr. Basi to Lily: Good work! A solid B on the classwork. You can write the final when you get home.

Mom to Lily: We miss you. Only 3 more weeks to go.

"Bring me another glass of wine," Damarais demands when the waiter stops to top up our water glasses the following afternoon. She's wearing a sleek beige pantsuit, chunky black jewelry and a Bluetooth in her ear. She looks like a cat ready to pounce, the way she watches the other tables.

"Of course." The waiter looks at me. "How is everything?"

My mouth is full of smoked-salmon tart, so I nod. Everything is perfect. Except for the chunk of salmon stuck in my teeth.

"So you see," Damarais says, "Trainer and Hill is ideally suited to represent you."

I know. And I'm thrilled. But I'm surprised at how few questions she's asked me. Mostly, she's talked about her other clients and how well they're doing.

She holds up her finger. "Excuse me." And she's back on her Bluetooth. Which is totally okay because now I can wiggle the piece of salmon out of my teeth.

"No, we will not settle for anything less," Damarais hisses. "That's our final offer. If they don't like it, they can shove it." The waiter delivers her second glass of wine. "I'm in the middle of something here, Holly. We'll talk later." She disconnects and reaches for her wine. "Where were we?"

"You were talking about my representation." I sound calm, but inside I am screaming with excitement.

"Right! You're the hot new thing. Look at how much press attention you've gotten in the last three weeks. And that's without representation." She winks. "Or at least *good* representation."

I can hardly believe it myself. Photos of Etienne and me at the Copper Awards. Press about my choice of dress. Plus the interview with the *Hollywood Slate*.

She slides a beige envelope across the table. "I'm delighted to present you with our agency contract. Of course, since you're a minor, we'll need your parents to sign off too. But this is your copy, Lily. Welcome to Trainer and Hill!"

I cannot speak. It's agency representation by the best of the best.

She sips more wine. "You're going to be a star, Lily. We're determined to take you to the top."

To the top. Hand trembling, I lift my tart. I put it back down. *You're going to be a star.* It's what I've wanted since, like, forever. Suddenly, everything around me sharpens. The clank of cutlery. The smell of garlic. The hard blue chair pressing into my knee. I will remember this moment for the rest of my life.

"Once you sign our contract, I'll follow up on the offers you told me about." I'd told Damarais everything when we first sat down, but I wasn't sure she'd heard, given how many times she stopped to take calls.

"Of course, you'll need to get some work done. We'll schedule everything for next month, when you're done shooting. I've booked your consult for late Thursday afternoon."

Huh? "What kind of work?"

"Breast implants certainly." She studies me over the rim of her glass. "Possibly butt implants. You told the *Hollywood Slate* you don't believe in surgery, but we do."

Panic rises. Surgery. Needles. Yuk. "But my parents—"

"I've already talked to them." She smiles. "Nic gave me their number. They're totally on board."

* * *

I Skype with my parents later that night. "Trainer and Hill is huge!" Mom says. She's at the kitchen table, her face flushed. "Your dad still doesn't like the idea of surgery, but between you, me and Damarais, he's outnumbered. Besides, Damarais says bust enhancement is a simple procedure these days. With a little help, she says you could be star material, Lily!"

I guess Damarais changed her mind about the butt implants, because she obviously hasn't mentioned them to my parents.

Dad is more subdued. "Is this what you really want?" he asks.

Suddenly restless, I jump up and look out the window. Down below, Los Angeles is a silvery web of streets and cars and high-rises. Joy thrums through my veins. A web of possibility. "Being an actress is all I've ever wanted. You know that."

"But the surgery?" he presses.

Who really wants surgery? Pulling my gaze from the window, I look back at my parents and sidestep the question. "Damarais is talking Academy Awards. Deals worth hundreds of thousands of dollars."

Mom laughs. "I know. I can hardly believe how fast things are moving."

Me either. Since lunch, I've been light-headed with giddiness.

"This is your dream come true, Lily. You've wanted to be an actress since you were three years old. I'm so pleased you have a shot at the

big time, because I know that's what you want."
She pauses, gives me a careful look. "But your
father's right. Surgery is a big step. You don't
have to do it. You can always say no."

"I'd probably do it eventually anyway. Why
wait?"

Dad nods, although he doesn't look partic-
ularly happy. "Your mother and I will fly down
on the weekend. We want to meet Damarais.
We need to give June a letter of termination too.
And thank her for all she's done for you."

That would be a great big zero. Unlike June,
Damarais sees my potential. She'll take me to the
very top. Which is where I want to be.

* * *

"Everybody does it," Ellen says on Wednesday
morning when I admit how much surgery scares
me. The makeup trailer is packed with people
getting ready for today's big scene. John is two
chairs down; Etienne is in the chair beside me.
"Some women make a career out of it," she adds.

"Don't," Etienne says when he catches my eye
in the mirror. "It's a bad move."

I laugh him off. "You're a guy. You don't understand." Ellen dabs foundation on my cheeks.

"No, *you* don't understand. It is just the beginning." Etienne's sexy-flirt look has been replaced by a thin-lipped grimness that startles me. "Soon they will want to make you over completely. They will want to change you inside and out." His words are clipped, very French.

"I know."

Etienne is wrong. Going through hell with his former business manager has left him paranoid. "Damarais just wants what's best for me," I say.

He opens his mouth, but the makeup artist takes a large powder brush to his face and he is forced to shut up.

That afternoon we shoot the turning-point scene with John and Brooklyn. It's a pivotal moment in which I confront Bill about his feelings for Kim, only I do it during the lunch rush and all hell breaks loose. During Thursday morning's shoot, Michael comes on to Iris again. Like I did the first time, I rebuff him. When we finish, I crack a joke with Etienne, but it's his turn to rebuff me. He doesn't even smile.

Damarais is on the phone when the car drops me outside a brick building in Beverly Hills late Thursday. I do a double take at the sight of the discreet gold sign: *Dr. Stuart Grainger, Plastic Surgeon.* It's necessary, I remind myself as I wave at Damarais. Everybody does it.

Signaling "one minute" with her finger, Damarais continues to pace and talk. "I don't care if Brooklyn is giving you grief!"

Brooklyn? There's only one Brooklyn I know.

"She needs to do what she's told." Her stilettos clack out an angry beat on the sidewalk. "You tell Brooklyn that if she doesn't smarten up, she can find other representation."

Whoa.

Damarais disconnects and gives me a tight smile. "Brooklyn Cory is such a bitch. Plus she's yesterday's news."

Maybe, but isn't an agent supposed to say good things about her clients?

She ushers me into a hushed waiting room with gray leather couches and seafoam-green walls. "Dr. Grainger is one of the best plastic surgeons in California. I'll wait here and we'll meet in his office later." She's back on her phone before I can respond.

The next half hour is a self-conscious blur. Dr. Grainger is young, wiry and quiet. Luckily, the middle-aged nurse who stays with us isn't. Her motherly chatter keeps me from being frozen with fear as the doctor examines me one body part at a time. "The photographs go on the computer," she explains when he starts taking pictures. "Dr. Grainger will reconstruct on the screen first, so you can be sure of the results."

After I'm dressed, the nurse escorts me down the hall to a large corner office. Dr. Grainger sits behind a sleek black desk. Damarais sits in front.

"Can't you go any bigger?" Damarais asks as I slide into the chair beside her. They're both staring into his computer monitor.

"Not with good results." Dr. Grainger tilts the screen so I can see. Shock ripples through me. There are my breasts. He presses a key. Larger breasts appear over my own. "I'll make the incision under here, so it won't be seen." He points.

Incision. Gross.

"The implants will go in there, mimicking your natural shape." He looks at me. "Does that work for you?"

I'm suddenly nauseated. Am I really doing this? I take a deep breath. "Yes."

Damarais squints at the image. "Are you sure you can't make them bigger?"

I gulp. They're already the size of melons.

"I could, but Lily is petite. Her breast size should stay proportional with her height and overall build. It won't look natural otherwise."

Thank God for that.

"What about the other procedures?" Damarais asks.

"Give me a minute." His fingers fly over the keys. "I need to pull up her face."

A sharp, metallic bitterness floods my mouth. "What other procedures?"

Thirteen

"Your face." Damarais stares at the screen. "We need to fix it too."

What does she mean, fix it?

When my face appears on the monitor, Dr. Grainger points to my cheeks. "She has great bone structure."

"Maybe." Damarais frowns. "But her nose needs to be thinned, and her eyes need to be widened."

The fries I ate for lunch cramp my stomach. I feel like I might throw up. I grip the edge of the chair and stare at myself. What's wrong with my eyes?

"The rhinoplasty will take care of the nose."

Rhinoplasty?

Click. Click. Click. With a few keystrokes, Dr. Grainger makes my nose narrower and straighter.

"What about the tip?" Damarais asks.

More clicking. The nose on the screen now has a cute, upturned end.

"As for the blepharoplasty, I can do the tops and bottoms of the lids at the same time." His fingers fly over the keyboard again.

Sweat trickles down my back. "You didn't say anything about my face the other day."

"I said you'd need work." She's still studying the screen. "That we'd schedule everything for next month." She points to the corner of my eye. "Wider there."

"You said my breasts. And maybe my butt."

"Your butt is fine for now."

For now. Nice.

"But your face is too Asian."

I freeze. Too Asian? I stare at her profile. Seriously?

"And Asian is in, but only nonthreatening, westernized Asian," she murmurs.

Westernized Asian. Isn't that what I am?

"If you're going to be represented by Trainer and Hill," she adds, "you need to modify your look."

Modify my look. Become more white. I clutch the edge of the chair so hard I'm surprised I don't

break a finger. All my life I've been too something. Too exotic. Too white. Too Asian. But this?
This is too weird.

"Yes!" Damarais exclaims. "That's perfect.
Now make the left eye look the same."

The fries I ate for lunch turn into a ball of
cement as Dr. Grainger clicks my familiar eyes
away. I look at Damarais. "Do my parents know
about this?" I can't believe they'd say yes.

"Other than the breast implants, I didn't go
into specifics." She's still staring at the screen.
"I said we'd talk more when they got to town."
She points to my face. "What about the cheek-
bones? With the wider eyes, they kind of disappear
now." Silently, the two of them study my image.

"We could take some fat from here"—he taps
the apple of my cheek—"and that would give us
this." A few more clicks, and my cheeks are hollow.

"Better," she says. "But now I don't like the
chin."

"Right."

They are talking about me like I'm a thing.
A piece of clay. A hunk of dough. Horrified,
I watch my image morph and change until I
barely recognize myself.

"Good work," Damarais murmurs. "Very nice."

It's not nice at all. I stare at the stranger looking back at me. I hate it.

And I have to live with myself.

"It's a good start," the doctor says. "She's still young, so modifications may be needed down the road."

Down the road. Oh god, Etienne was right. A wave of dizziness rocks me. It will never end. "I'm not sure about the face thing." My voice seems to come from somewhere far away.

Dr. Grainger looks at me. "It's entirely your decision. I certainly won't do anything you're not comfortable with."

"There's nothing to worry about, Lily." Damarais waves my concern away. "The pain is minimal, right, doctor?"

"I wouldn't call it minimal, but we do have pain medication, yes." He continues to look at me.

"You'll have round-the-clock care," Damarais adds. "And Trainer and Hill will pay for everything."

"But it's my face we're talking about." After years of always finding fault with it, I'm not sure I want to change it.

Damarais's sharp dark eyes bore into me. "I told you the other day, Lily, you have all the makings of a star. But you can't afford to be type-cast. You need a more homogenized look."

June said the same thing. Suddenly shivering, I wrap my arms around my middle. "But my looks got me the role of Iris."

She gives me an Ice Queen smile. "And it's a good start. But it's only that. You need to trust me on this, Lily. You're paying us to represent you, remember?"

Tell Brooklyn that if she doesn't smarten up, she can find other representation.

If I say no, Damarais won't represent me. And I can't operate in Hollywood without an agent. I want a good one. I want her. "What if we do my breasts now and my face down the road?" I'm grasping at straws, desperate. This is the biggest opportunity of my life, and I don't want to let it go.

"No." Damarais shakes her head. "You're the hot new thing right now. The flavor of the week. You need to take advantage of it."

Hot new thing? Flavor of the week? My heart lurches. I haven't invested all this time to flame out in a year. "I don't want to be the hot new thing. I'm in this for the long haul."

Damarais clucks her tongue. "It's just a figure of speech."

I gaze at the person on the screen. An ache goes through me. Mom's eyes are gone. Dad's chin is gone. I'm gone. I may not always know who I am, but I know who I'm not. And I'm not that. "I can't do it."

"What do you mean?"

Despair, black and bottomless, threatens to swallow me whole. I can't believe I just said it. My dream is over. Dead in the water. Gonzo. "I can't change my face." My voice comes out strangled. I'm numb. Stunned. It's the right choice, I know it, but a part of me still shrivels and dies.

Damarais pats my hand. "We'll talk," she says.

I pull my hand away. "There's nothing to talk about." If I can't make it in Hollywood with the face I was born with, then I won't make it at all. "I've decided."

Fourteen

Claire to Lily: You told Damarais what?????????
Dad to Lily: Tickets are paid for. We're coming anyway.
Lily to Sean Tribley: I have your money.

"Y ou come to town and get involved in everybody else's business, but who are you to pass judgment on my guitar playing?" Etienne's character, Michael, is yelling at Iris.

His angry words ricochet around the studio and make me tremble. There's a collective hush as everybody waits for me to deliver my lines. It's a pivotal scene, and I'm managing, but just barely. Yesterday with Damarais gutted me. Saying no to her was the hardest thing I've ever done.

"I'm not passing judgment," I say. "You just think I am. It's your own fear of judgment that's crippling you. And fear of your own talent. You're afraid it will take you places and leave the people you love behind."

A vein pops in his neck. "How dare you." Instinctively, I recoil. His anger feels so real. "You don't know me. You don't have the answers. And what are *you* running from, Iris?" His blue eyes bore into me. "Who are you, anyway?"

The lights are so hot, I'm feeling faint. Who am I? I've asked that question since I was old enough to look into the mirror and know I was different. Maybe it's the wrong question. Maybe the question isn't who am I, but who do I want to be? Deep down, when I'm not acting?

"It doesn't matter who I am. What matters is that I'm right."

I turn and walk the dozen feet to my mark. Saying no to Damarais was also right. Too bad it feels so wrong.

"Cut!" Nic hollers. "That's a wrap!"

Conversation starts; someone laughs. I walk a few more feet, needing to get away from the harsh heat of the lights. From Etienne's anger. But he follows me.

"Good job," he says.

I turn around. Even in his geeky shirt and Value Village jeans, he is totally gorgeous. "You were right about Damarais," I say. My anger, which has been simmering since yesterday, boils to the surface. "She didn't want me to change my name, but she wanted me to get new boobs and an entirely new face. Happy now?"

"What did you tell her?"

Tears feather the back of my throat. "What do you think I told her?" Brooklyn saunters by and smirks. Etienne just stares at me, waiting. I swallow and say, "I told her no, okay? I turned her down."

He steps closer. Even after hours on the set, he still smells delicious. "You might think you regret it now, but you won't later. Your face is perfect. You're perfect. You start chipping away at that and you lose your soul. It happened to me. Luckily, I found my way back." He glances at Brooklyn. "But not everybody does."

It's easy for Etienne. He's A-list now. He's forgotten what it's like to be starting out. Despair slams me. Plus, his looks work in his favor.

"Hey, Lily," Nic yells. "There's someone here to see you."

It's Pat Landsberg, striding across the studio. She stops in front of us and smiles. "Good afternoon, Lily. We need to talk."

* * *

"You turned Damarais down but you still want us to write the termination letter to June?" Mom says after they arrive at Uncle Mike's and we're sitting at the dining room table. She shakes her head. "I don't understand. What happened?"

I grip my soda. "It doesn't matter."

You need a more homogenized look.

Maybe surgery would have made me easier to cast, but easy isn't always better. Changing my face would have been selling out. I couldn't do it. And I can't talk about it with my parents yet either. It's too painful.

Mom studies me carefully. "The sparkle is gone from your eyes. I don't like to see that."

"I'm tired. It's been a long week." I tap the script Pat gave me. "This will make it better." I look at Dad. "You'll call June, right? And the lawyer after that?"

Yesterday at the studio, Pat was highly critical of June. I don't think she likes Damarais much either. When I told her I'd turned Hill and Taylor down, she suggested I forget about having an agent. She told me to hire a good entertainment lawyer instead. She gave me the name of a lawyer she trusts and then handed me a script. "We want you to play Meagan," she'd said. "It's an amazing part about the daughter of a congresswoman. Meaty and deep. The kind of role that doesn't come along often. Especially for a newcomer."

"Pat's contract is complex. Maybe June should take a look at it," Mom says to Dad.

"No!"

In unison, their heads pivot to me. "June knows about the role of Meagan," I admit. "She asked Pat to cast another one of her clients instead."

Dad's mouth drops open.

Mom's eyes widen. "Really?"

I nod. "Yeah. And she hasn't been around much these last few weeks either. She's been busy meeting with casting directors and doing stuff for her other clients."

"No wonder you have issues with her." Mom looks at Dad. "Lily's right. We need to terminate her contract."

I don't want to think about June. I slide the script across the table. "You should read this. It's a great story."

Dad gulps the last of his tea. "If you take this on, you'd be shooting in Washington for over two months."

"I know." And that's the catch. We don't know anybody in DC. "But opportunities like this don't come along every day. And I know I said the same thing about the role of Iris, but it's true. I can't turn down good offers this early in my career."

And it is a career, and I'm in it for the long haul, but I'm still a newbie and I need to make smart choices about roles.

Mom looks at Dad again. "Mother could fly down and stay with Mike. I could go with Lily. Be her chaperone."

Mom would do that?

"With the amount of money they're offering, I could take a temporary leave of absence from work," she adds. "Lily can afford to pay me to act as manager for a couple of months."

Mom's right. The fee is huge. Massive.

"We could rent a temporary apartment," Mom adds. "It'll be summer. Lily won't have school, so the timing works well. You could join us after. We've never seen the east coast before."

Dad clears his throat. "Let me make some calls." He picks up the script. "And we'll need to read this. Without an agent, Lily needs us looking out for her."

No one will care about your career as much as you, Etienne had said. He was right about lots of things, but he was wrong about that. I jump up to hug Mom and Dad. My parents care as much as I do.

* * *

An hour later, I'm standing in front of the closet, wrapped in a fluffy bath towel and trying to decide what to wear for dinner out, when there's a knock on the door.

"Come in."

It's Samantha, white mug in hand and wearing the ugliest green sweatshirt ever created. "You owe me two hundred and fifty dollars. Some guy named Sean came by and—"

"Ssssh!" I yank her into the room.

"Watch the coffee," she screeches, holding her mug up.

I slam the door and retrieve my robe from the bathroom. When I come out, she's in the easy chair, her feet propped up on the bed. "He says you were supposed to meet him here at seven last night."

I was, but by the time I finished with Pat and got home, it was after eight. And Sean was the last thing on my mind.

Samantha's eyes are unreadable over the rim of her white mug. "He says you were paying him to do your math homework."

I retrieve my purse. "Yeah, and if you tell my parents, I swear I will kill you."

"Seriously." She smirks. "You paid him?"

"Yeah, I paid him and I feel rotten about it, but please don't tell my parents," I plead. "I'll tell them myself. They need to hear it from me."

I'm not sure when I'll tell them—maybe at dinner, maybe when we get home—but I will. I hand her the money I'd set aside for Sean. "You might be a math whiz, but I'm only half Asian. I don't do numbers."

Startled, she stops her mug midway to her mouth. I brace myself. Here it comes. In her eyes, I'm not Asian at all.

"You think because I'm full I can do math?" She snorts. "Science, yeah, but not math. Mom's had a tutor on retainer since I was ten." She runs a finger around the rim of her mug. "It must be a family thing if numbers mess us both up."

A family thing. Warmth unfurls in my belly. I cannot believe she has said it.

She averts her gaze, picks at a stray thread on her ugly green sweatshirt. "I could show you some stuff. I mean, if you want. You don't have to, but numbers are numbers anywhere, and the tutor showed me some tricks." Her cheeks are flushed when she finally looks up. "But if you want to do it yourself—I mean, with Sean—that's okay too. I totally get it."

Sam's nervous, I suddenly realize. Not snotty but shy. "Sure," I say. Because I still have to write the final. And now that shooting's nearly done, I owe it to myself, and to my parents, to at least try. "That would be great."

"Cool." She gulps more coffee. "Mom said—" She stops. "I wonder—" She stops again. "Could I come watch a shoot? I'm on reading break next week. Mom said she'd drive me. Would that be okay?"

The warmth spreads through me. "Of course. My mom and dad are coming Monday. Come with them."

"Great." She fidgets with her hair. "Do you think you could...I mean, I kind of wonder... would you introduce me to Etienne Quinn?"

There's a crazed, dazed fangirl look in her eyes. So like me. I smile. "For sure."

She blushes. "He's, like, totally hot."

I grin. "The hottest thing since fire. Plus, he smells."

She wrinkles her nose. "Smells?"

"Like maple-sugar bacon."

She frowns.

"He does." I start to laugh. "And seriously, it's the best smell in the world."

LAURA LANGSTON is the author of *Last Ride, Hannah's Touch* and *Exit Point* in the Orca Soundings series, as well as teen novels and picture books. Laura lives in Victoria, British Columbia.